BLACK LIGHT: CUFFED

MEASHA STONE

Published by Black Collar Press

Black Light: Cuffed
Measha Stone

EBook 978-0-9982191-5-8
Print 978-0-9982191-7-2

Cover Art by Eris Adderly, http://erisadderly.com/

This book is a work of fiction. Names, characters, places, and incidents either are products of the author's imagination or are used fictitiously. Any resemblance to actual persons, living or dead, events, or locales is entirely coincidental.

This story takes place in the Black Light world created by Livia Grant and Jennifer Bene. Measha Stone graciously accepted the invitation to play in our naughty world and we thank her from the bottom of our hearts for lending us her talent by joining the Black Collar family.

First Electronic Publish Date, April 2017

First Print Publish Date, July 2017

❀ Created with Vellum

BLACK LIGHT SERIES

*L*awyers went into divorce litigation to avoid cases like this. Sydney Richards sat back in her plush office chair and tossed her ballpoint pen on top of the file. She wanted to drag her hands through her hair, but the tightly wound bun sitting on top of her head wouldn't allow for it.

Groaning, she pushed away from her desk.

This case would be the death of her sanity if she let it. And it didn't look like there was much choice. *When life gives you lemons, make some lemonade,* her mother used to say. Well, what the hell do you do when life hands you two dead girls and what looked like a rushed arrest?

"Sydney?" The door to her office opened and Denise poked her head in, scanning the room. Finding Sydney pacing along her bookshelves she finished stepping in and closed the door. "I just wanted to remind you about the charity dinner tomorrow night. You bought tickets at the Christmas party. It's for the Women's Shelters of D.C." She tapped her hand-held device with a steno pen. Most likely checking off the reminder from a to-do list. Which is why Sydney had Denise, she made to-do lists and checked things off of them. Sydney had multiple homicide cases that would keep her up at night.

"Tomorrow? Really?" A night of long speeches and elevator music was not how she wanted to start the weekend. "Is there an auction or anything like that being held at the dinner?"

"No auction, but there are, of course, donations being taken. Aside from the five-hundred-dollar dinner ticket you purchased — for yourself and a guest." Denise didn't bother hiding her smile. There would be no guest.

"Do you have plans tomorrow night?" Sydney asked.

Denise laughed. "I may have failed to mention there's going to be a band. The band Perry is performing."

"You don't have to keep convincing me; I already don't want the tickets," Sydney said with a smile. Denise worked her ass off keeping up with Sydney's schedule and all the last-minute changes like this one. "Take them if you want, and make a donation for me while you're there. You have my card."

"Are you sure you don't want them? You've been working yourself to the bone this week," Denise said.

"Yes, I'm sure," Sydney replied. "Please take them, have fun."

"Well, if you're sure. I'd love to. Thank you!"

"Of course, you've worked yourself just as crazy as I have these past weeks, and I don't see it letting up anytime soon. This Michael Stanley case isn't sitting right with me."

Sydney sighed and leaned back against the shelves. "Can you set up a meeting with the detectives that are working the case? If we are going to file the charges tomorrow, I need to ask them a few questions."

"An email came in this afternoon. The lead Detective, Mr. Steinbeck, had a heart attack and is in the hospital. Permanent leave or something like that. Detective Tate took over as lead, he'll be working with Detective Trainer from now on. I'll get it all set up." A quick nod and she was off.

Tate. Sydney's head jerked up at the sound of those four letters pushed together. She knew a Tate. A flash of renewed irritation and embarrassment rushed through her body and her face heated. Damn him. She wasn't going to blush thinking about that night, about those things he'd said. She was at work, and she needed to focus. She was an assistant DA for Christ sake!

"You okay?" Denise walked back in, holding a piece of paper in her hand. Sydney hadn't moved an inch from where her paralegal had left her.

"Yes. I'm fine," Sydney said, finding her feet and moving back over to her desk to gather the files. "Just tired." Now there was an understatement. The case had been keeping her up nights for over a week. The detectives had kept her in the loop on most of their findings as they dug through the evidence, and most of it gave her nightmares.

Now they had made an arrest and she found herself digging through the rest of the reports slowly trickling in. From what she could see so far, there wasn't much pointing to any one person, but Detective Steinbeck's partner, Detective Trainer, had messaged her the day before saying he was taking Michael Stanley in for questioning.

By this morning, he'd managed to get an arrest warrant and put the man behind bars. It was now up to her to figure out what to charge him with and get the process going toward trial. Only, she wasn't sure Detective Trainer had given enough thought to all the evidence.

Michael Stanley may have been the convenient arrest, but he might not have been the correct one.

The stress of having to prep for an arraignment when she wasn't a hundred percent convinced of the guilt of the defendant weighed on her. Tension built in her body and her mind reeled with worries. Sending an innocent man to jail couldn't happen, not by her hand.

"You want to grab a drink? The day's long done." Denise gestured to the darkness outside the office windows.

"No, thanks." Sydney stuffed her files into her briefcase. She knew where she wanted to go, what she needed to do to get the stress and kinks out of her muscles. "I'm just going to go home and soak in a hot bath." The locks snapped closed on the leather-bound briefcase.

"That sounds nice, too."

Sydney noticed the somber expression cross over Denise's face as she turned to leave, her shoulders a little more slumped than usual. They hadn't gone out for an after-work drink in months, not since Sydney had found herself a new playground. One she could rely on to keep her identity from leaking outside the doors for all of D.C.'s elite society to examine and use against her. She had a real shot at becoming district attorney if she could just keep her nose clean, and win a big case.

Like the Michael Stanley case.

She didn't need distractions. And the memory of something dark and delicious that would never come into the light was only a distraction.

One evening meant to be a fun, voyeuristic escape quickly turned into a blind date. And with a man she'd been drooling over since seeing him for the first time at the club. It all seemed so surreal, so perfect. He'd even been everything she'd hoped, so dark and unbending. Until it was time for him to bend, and he didn't. Accusations and assumptions were thrown, and in the end, she wound up heading home in a sour mood.

A bad mood that the Stanley case expanded to an almost unbearable point.

Until she could get face to face with Detective Trainer and have her questions answered, she was at a standstill.

Zipping up her coat to help ward off the March air, she glanced around her office to see if she'd forgotten something. Phone: in purse. Purse: draped off her elbow. Brief case: in hand. Nope. Got everything.

Flicking off the lights to her office, she let out another ragged sigh. The floor was near empty. Most of the attorneys had already retired to the bar downstairs or gone home.

Sydney hadn't lied to Denise. Not exactly. She needed to sink herself into something all right, but a hot bath wasn't exactly what she had in mind.

CHAPTER 2

*J*ate watched a woman being tied to the St. Andrew's Cross on the circular platform with unusual disinterest. Maybe it was the way her dom mishandled the ropes, making it too easy for the sub to slip out of the binds and simply walk away from him. He usually held more patience for the newer doms. The man obviously had been taught some tricks of the trade, but he simply lacked experience.

Deciding the last thing the couple needed was his judgmental stare on them while they had their fun, he turned and walked through the dungeon looking for something, or someone, to interest him. He'd taken the same walk at least a dozen times over the past weeks, and nothing even tempted him to a second glance.

His body needed a release. The tensions building at work and the irritation of his personal life were beginning to weigh him down. He'd come to Black Light thinking to meet someone to help him work off his angst at least for an evening, but it was a dumbass thought. Everywhere he looked he realized he wasn't looking for someone new, he was checking to see if *she* was there.

The damn woman who in one single evening managed to get her hooks so deep into him, he'd spent the last few weeks trying to forget her. In the past, a new flavor often washed the taste of the old away, but it wasn't working this time. Now, even looking at another woman in the club only made him wonder how long she would hide from him. She hadn't given him the impression of being so skittish.

Their evening at Valentine Roulette hadn't given either of them a happily ever after, but it hadn't been as bad as she'd stalked off thinking. She'd taken everything he had said and twisted it around until she'd gotten herself so wound up he couldn't get through to her anymore. Not exactly off to a great start, he had to admit, but he wasn't finished with her. The woman had more spunk and class than he'd seen in any submissive he'd played with lately.

Thinking a drink would help him at least relax, he headed to the bar and ordered up an old fashioned. The hum of the dungeon continued to fill the air around him. The yelps, cries, and guttural sounds of hard fucking going on between the spanks and the slaps all turned into background music as he sipped his drink.

The bartender leaned across the bar with a mischievous smile. The purple hue from the black-lights highlighted her cleavage the more she leaned toward him, but other than noticing, it did nothing for him. "I think the girl you've been waiting on has finally shown her face." She gave a wink, and twirled a pigtail between her fingers.

"Becca, I'm not waiting on anyone." It took physical strength to keep from turning around to see where she was pointing with her gaze. He gripped his glass a little harder, and forced a wider grin onto his lips.

"Uh, huh." She winked and turned her back on him. "Except I saw you with her on Valentine's Day and haven't seen you with another woman since. That's not like you," she said over her shoulder and sashayed off toward another customer.

Not like him at all, he'd have to agree. At thirty-two he hadn't found anyone to settle down with, much to his mother's dismay.

7

There was plenty of time to find the right woman, and he wasn't settling for anything less than everything he wanted. Problem was, most of the women he found in the scene wanted playtime but didn't want to carry it outside the bedroom. Or if they did, they weren't into his particular brand of dominant/submissive relationship.

"You waited too long," Becca said in her singsong voice as she walked past him toward the other end of the bar and another patron.

He didn't even try to ignore the comment. He turned around on the stool to find Sydney, the woman who had been successfully evading him for weeks, walking towards the spanking benches with a man following close behind her. Dominick. Tate had seen him play a few times with various subs. He wasn't one for serious play. A few slaps on the ass and then he jumped right to the fucking. The man didn't have the self-control to finish a scene before burying his cock into his sub.

Sydney didn't public fuck, though.

Oh, she probably thought Valentine Roulette was the first time he'd noticed her, but she was wrong. So far, she'd proved to have a knack for jumping to the wrong conclusions when it came to him. He'd noticed her plenty of times, and seeing her stag it at the Valentine's Day event gave him a chance to get to know her. It hadn't been a hard decision, offering to share a table at the Roulette game to watch the scenes play out around them. It wasn't completely unplanned either, to snag her before someone else did. And now that he had, he didn't like seeing someone like Dominick pointing her toward a spanking bench.

"Down boy." Chase Cartwright, supermodel turned club owner, laughed and patted Tate on his shoulder. "You look ready to launch yourself into some rescue mission." He leaned back against the bar.

"I'm fine," tension caused his jaw to clench so tight, Tate could barely utter even those two simple words.

Chase laughed. "Uh huh, and I'm too tired to go back upstairs and help Jaxson with our Emma tonight." He grinned and gestured toward the scene Tate glared at. "Isn't that the girl you wanted me to track down for you?"

"Yes." Tate nodded.

"Still mad because I wouldn't give you her last name?"

"No." Tate glanced at him from the corner of his eye. "I get it."

"I'm guessing you never got a hold of her. Is this the first time you're seeing her since Valentine's Day?"

"Yes." Tate nodded again, keeping his eyes fixed on Sydney and the jackass trying to take control of the scene.

"Do you think you can behave? Emma really is waiting for me upstairs. Jaxson wanted me to come down and get the paddle he left down here earlier."

Tate forced his muscles to relax and leaned back against the bar. "You have this whole club, why play upstairs in your condo?" A bit forward, but if Tate owned the club, he wouldn't be playing in a bedroom on the top floor of the club, he'd be playing inside it.

"Not playing tonight." His expression hardened. "I had hoped, but our Emma had other ideas."

"Right." Tate knew exactly what he was talking about, and he wasn't too proud of a man to admit he envied what Chase and Jaxson had with Emma. A real relationship. No game playing, no dancing around their wants. Everyone knew their place, knew their role, and through bad or good moments they could always count on each other.

"Try to have a good one." Chase patted him on the shoulder and headed off into the crowd of people.

Tate's eyes drifted back over to the spanking bench. The little distraction had made him miss the part where Sydney had pulled up her skirt and climbed onto the bench. She faced his direction, her bare ass pointed away from him. The lighting in the room cast a bit of a shadow over her face, but he could still make out her expression pretty clearly.

9

Complete boredom.

Dominick was already swinging away at her ass with his bare hand and rubbing his erection through his faux leather pants. If Sydney didn't fall asleep first, he might get his cock out of his pants before she hopped off the table. Had she even taken the time to talk to him before she headed over to the bench with him? Or did she just pick the first guy who offered to spank her and go forth without negotiation or even a short conversation? Though he doubted she would even be fully honest if she had taken the time to discuss their scene.

His ire quickly began to get the best of him. She was a big girl, he reminded himself, and if she was there in the club she knew the scene. He'd seen her play with other doms before. She wasn't a novice. Although it had occurred to him on more than one occasion that she had a really hard time expressing what she wanted, because she rarely seemed satisfied.

Dominick moved behind her, his hand disappearing between her legs. Tate's jaw tightened, and he started to push away from his seat when Sydney bucked up and twisted around. Too far away to hear what she was saying, he could only assume it effectively shut down Dominick's plans. While the novice dom looked irritated by what she was saying, he backed away with a nod.

Tate watched from the bar area as Dominick helped her off the spanking bench and finished speaking with her before she turned and walked away. To his credit, Dominick bounced back rather quickly and shuffled off, back on the prowl, only looking back once as Sydney left him behind.

When Tate turned back to find where Sydney had gone to, he couldn't locate her. Had she given up so easily and left? Those little taps to her ass couldn't have sated her need for a spanking.

"A sweet red, please." A soft voice called to the bartender from a few stools down.

"Sweet like candy?" he asked before he could get his mind in line.

Sydney jerked to the side, staring at him with a surprised look. "I like sweet wine. Is that a problem?" A perfectly shaped eyebrow raised and her hand rested on her pushed out hip. Someone was looking for another sparring match.

He wasn't playing into it this time. If she wanted it, she'd have to ask for it.

"Not at all. Didn't really peg you for a merlot type of woman." He forced himself to sound casual as he moved alongside the bar.

She didn't respond. She just stared up at him, making him guess her thoughts. One moment she looked as though she were going to give him a snarky answer, the next she looked defeated. Well, that wouldn't do.

"Your scene didn't last very long." He commented as he dug out some cash to pay for her drink. She tried to shoo his hand away, but he managed to hand the bills over before she succeeded.

"No. It didn't." She nodded and lifted her glass of red wine to her lips. He watched as the red liquid disappeared into her mouth, his balls tightening with hope his cock would be following at some point. And soon.

Tate watched her trying her damnedest to ignore him. The soft glow of the lighting around the bar exposed the gentleness of her features. Her dark hair was pulled back into a bun almost giving her a serious look, but he'd gotten to know her pretty well at the roulette game, and serious didn't suit her.

"Have you been avoiding Black Light all together or just me?" He decided to go at her full steam.

She met his gaze with surprise that quickly morphed into a smirk. "Yes, I've been working myself silly trying to drown out the memory of you." The mocking wasn't going to get her very far with him, but maybe that's what she wanted.

"Work been busy?" They hadn't gotten too specific about their work when they had met, keeping their conversation mostly about the game and their own kinks.

She finished her wine and motioned for a second. "Yes. And I wanted to sort of put it out of my mind tonight, so if you'll just go away so a real man can step up, that'd be great."

His eyebrows shot up, and he could feel the muscles in his forehead tense at her boldness.

"So no more little shots and brattiness, just going straight for rude and obnoxious. Hoping that will get you the hard spanking you're desperately looking for tonight?" He moved closer to her, but was careful not to touch her. When Becca came back around with the bottle of wine, he reached over and covered her glass with his hand.

"What are you doing?" She craned her neck to look up at him, a mixture of annoyance and hope lingering in the heated stare.

"I'm asking you what you want; it's a direct question. If you came here looking for someone to give you that hard spanking you seem to need, I'm offering my hand. If you want me to walk away and let you try to find the next guy who will give you a few unsatisfying swats, I'll walk right now. Either way, if you're playing tonight you're not having another glass." He should have just walked away. Just let her wallow in her own stress puddle and let her figure out what she needed, but he couldn't. Just wouldn't walk away.

For a moment, he didn't think she'd answer. Then she seemed to regain control over herself and rolled her eyes. "Whatever," she muttered and released her hold on the glass. Becca giggled and walked away.

As a sign, it seemed positive. Deciding to press his luck, he leaned against the bar, crowding her smaller frame even more. "So, what's your decision?" A lone piece of hair ran down the back of her neck, and he resisted the urge to wrap it around his finger and tug.

She looked up at him with narrowed eyes. "Fine. You want to put your hands on me, let's go." She turned around in a rush and took a few steps in the direction of the play areas before he managed to get his hand wrapped around her arm.

"Oh, you have no idea how much I've wanted to get my hands on you."

* * *

IT FINALLY HAPPENED. She lost her mind completely. Sydney looked up at the man half dragging her toward the spanking benches. She'd just been there, just done that, and the act had only left her wanting more. More of everything, except what Dominick had to offer. That ass actually thought a dozen half-strength swats was enough to qualify as an actual scene. The bird-brain actually thought he was going to just fuck her right there in the dungeon. Yeah. *No.* At least he'd been civil about her rejection.

Tate was different. The man appeared to be the very definition of control. The evening they'd spent at Roulette had shown her exactly how much that was true. His natural dominance had been one of the points of the evening that nagged her late at night when she tried her best to shove him from her mind.

You don't have to brat your way into a spanking, you can just ask. She'd huffed at his comment, and had ignored him for a few minutes until he had tried talking with her again. Now, here she was being led over to the same spanking bench he'd threatened her with only a few weeks ago.

Once they reached the available bench, he stopped and turned to her, dropping his hard grip on her bicep. Her head came up to his chin, making looking at his face impossible when he was so close. Instead of staring at his chest, his perfectly sculpted and, thanks to the tight t-shirt he wore, easily seen chest, she took a step back to look up at him.

His dark blue eyes examined her. The pencil skirt she'd worn to work that morning had been swapped out for a flirty pleated black skirt. And the hem was much shorter than anything she would dare wear to the office.

"Your blouse is wet." He pointed to her chest.

She cursed when she looked down. The bench hadn't been dried from the cleaning solution before Dominick had her bend over it. In such a hurry to find her release, she hadn't bothered to check either. Now her favorite white blouse was ruined. Blotches of the solution were all over it.

"The damn cleaning stuff." She wiped at the stains with her fingertips, as though that would help, and heaved a heavy sigh when she gave up. She'd come to Black Light to let off steam, to find her peaceful mind, and all she'd found so far was annoyance.

"I'll wipe it down, you can start getting undressed. No skirt, no panties, and you might as well take the blouse off, too." He didn't wait for her approval, he just turned and stalked off for the spray and paper towels.

She tried to conjure up irritation, or at least a smart-ass remark for him, but she couldn't ignore the warmth spreading over her at his obvious dominance. Not letting her have that second glass of wine, leading her by the arm to the spanking bench, and then just ordering her out of her clothes. Her frayed nerves started to soothe out beneath his presence.

By the time he got back, she was stripped down to her panties. "It's a thong." She pointed out and turned to wiggle her ass at him.

He lifted an eyebrow. "So?"

"So, I don't need to take them off." She shrugged and dropped her hands to her sides. She'd kicked off her heels and put them with her skirt, making her another inch shorter than him. The man must have really eaten his Wheaties as a child; he was fucking huge.

He folded his arms over his chest and widened his stance, not for one second easing up on the intense glare. "Tell me why you think when I tell you to take off your panties, you think it's okay not to. Thong or not."

She huffed a small laugh, suddenly very grateful she hadn't taken off her bra yet. Standing up for oneself was easier to do when one was at least somewhat clothed.

"Well, you want to get to my ass, right? So, with a thong you can."

He ran his tongue over his teeth beneath his closed lips, but didn't speak.

"It's just common sense." She tried again.

His nostrils flared the tiniest bit when he grunted.

"You don't need my thong off to spank my butt." She tried to find a stance to mimic his, but everything she tried only made her feel smaller under his stare.

"One more try, then this turns more into discipline than fun for you." His deep voice didn't rise in volume, but her cheeks heated with the obvious chastisement.

"If this is supposed to be for fun, it's not really working. Maybe I *am* too much for you." Her defenses went up, and she moved to grab her skirt from next to the bench. She'd been stupid. This was so stupid.

"Are you crying red?" His voice shook her, so demanding and unyielding.

"Look—"

He moved so quickly she didn't have a chance to step out of his way. His large hands were on her shoulders, his chest pressing up against her. She twisted enough to look up at him. His nose almost touching hers as he crouched down. The darkness of his eyes startled her just enough to keep her quiet.

"I think we negotiated pretty well at the roulette game, but if there's something you want to add to what I already know, now's the time to tell me. And if you think I can't handle your attitude, or you, I'll have that misconception cleared up within the hour. But if you really want to walk out you'll have to use your damn safeword. And bratting isn't a safeword."

She swallowed hard as her heart pounded out a Metallica melody in her chest. Words failed her. She'd dreamt for weeks of having his hands on her, his eyes boring into her with such intensity and here it was.

She gave a little shake of her head.

"Good. Now." He released her and squatted down, hooking his thumbs into the thin straps of her thong and yanked it down to her ankles. "Step out," he said. She barely realized her body was obeying him before it was done.

He stood back up, tucking the panties into his back pocket and snapped the shoulder strap of her bra. "Your tits are safe tonight, you can keep this on."

She nodded again, wondering where the hell her tongue went.

"Now, you clean the bench, while I go to my cubby. I don't think what I had originally planned is going to work."

After he walked away, she went about doing what he'd ordered. He'd dropped the spray and towels on the bench, and she had cleaned it all down and put the spray back before he returned. And when he did, her ass clenched.

A fraternity paddle. She wasn't a fan of wood. She'd told him that at the roulette game.

He placed the paddle on the bench and went over to her, running his hands over her shoulders and down her arms. The action calmed her enough to finally be able to focus on what was going to happen.

"You need some stress release, is that right, Sydney?" The sound of her name in his voice could have doubled as a love sonnet. "Work has been overwhelming? You've been letting your-self get all balled up because you didn't want to run into me here, is that right?"

It wasn't fair, using her own thoughts against her like that.

"Works been a bitch, yeah." She nodded.

His jaw clenched but he didn't chastise her for the cursing. "And you've been avoiding me."

"Not..." She decided to give him the truth. "Okay, so I didn't want to run into you."

"Good girl. See not so hard, right?" He smiled and the soft warmth already building burst into a flame inside her chest.

"Now, keep being my good girl and bend over the bench. There's handles on this one, grab them and hold on. Use your colors if you need them." He slipped his fingers to entwine with hers and turned her to the bench, helping her get into position.

The cool leather of the bench pressed against her half naked chest. Reaching to the sides, she found the handles and wrapped her fingers around them, gripping them tightly as his fingers started to run down the bare flesh of her ass.

"You hate wood." He leaned over her, talking quietly into her ear. "So, you'll get five of the paddle after I've given you what you've been looking for. One day you'll just come out and ask me, but for today, we'll just get that stress worked out of your body."

One day?

The first slap of his hand came as her mind tried to wrap around his insinuation. The second came directly after that. Hard swats. The man didn't need a paddle, his hand worked just fine! She grunted with the third and by the time she'd lost count, she wiggled beneath his punishing hand.

"Ow!" She yelled out, looking over her shoulder at him, ready to glare at him. He ignored her. Moving to stand on the left side of her, he wrapped one heavy arm around her waist and yanked her down the length of the bench, until her ass was higher in the air.

The hot sting she was already combating in her mind doubled as he intensified the spanking. The swats were harder and more spread out, so she couldn't evade him with his arm pinning her to him. She gripped the handles tighter, and realized the yelling she heard was coming from her.

"There we are." He patted her softly on the thighs and then delivered five stinging slaps to the same spot. She bucked up at the new fire, but quickly flattened herself again when he started to soothe the area with the tips of his fingers.

"Can't be uneven," he proclaimed before repeating the action on her right thigh.

She cried out and bucked up again, but he didn't even try to stop her, just continued with the slaps until he was finished and waited for her to get back into proper position before he soothed the area.

A deep calmness started to take over her body, the peaceful hum unraveled the tension of the day better than any glass of wine or hot bath could manage.

"See, you can be such a good girl." He cooed into her ear, his hand flat on her back. "Do you want more?" he asked.

Her mouth was dry, and she realized she had been panting. Her ass was on fire, but still she craved another round. Almost to her happy place, and a dozen or more from him would get her there.

"You have to ask, Sydney. You have to tell me what you want." He urged her, rubbing her back with his hand.

Her jaw clenched, the words in her throat, but unwilling to surface.

"Those little swats are what you call a spanking?" Her inner soul groaned at her words.

Tate laughed. "Okay then." He patted her shoulder and walked around her. "We'll skip it."

She rested her forehead on the bench, mentally kicking herself. Tate had already said he wouldn't cave to her bratting, so why did she insist on pushing it?

"You're wet, Sydney. So wet." His fingers were spreading her pussy lips wide, and one fingertip swiped across her clit making her jump. "I think I'd like to see you come."

Two fingers slipped inside of her and instead of reminding him she didn't fuck in public, she found herself pushing back against his hand. His second hand reached between her legs and began stroking her clit, rolling it, pinching it and rubbing it until she was fucking his fingers like someone who had no fucking control.

"There you go, that's good. Fuck, you're tight." He started to thrust his fingers into her, meeting her own movements. "Your clit is so tender, I see how you jump when I pinch it. You like that. The bite of pain." He pinched it again, and she spiraled out of control.

"Ah!" She screamed, her eyes widened, her mouth dry from hanging open as her entire body convulsed and her pussy clenched around his fingers. She screamed with each new wave, and they kept coming because he kept stroking her.

Finally, he pulled out of her passage, dragging his wet fingers over her ass to wipe them off before coming around the bench and placing a kiss to her forehead. "So beautiful. You are so perfect, my Sydney." He kissed her again and straightened up. Feeling hazy and weak, she rested against the bench, dropping her hands from the handles and sinking into the floating sensation he'd given her. Her ass still burned, her pussy now throbbing from the fingering he'd gifted her with. She just wanted to sink into the leather and enjoy the feelings.

"Now. About your disobedience."

The wood paddle connected with her ass, and she bounced upward from the horrid sting. He held her around her middle again, but she didn't flatten down. She stayed up on her knees with him holding her while he delivered the four remaining strokes, rapid and hard.

"Tate," she yelled, "no!"

"No?" He pressed the wooden paddle against her ass. "When you disobeyed me, and kept that thong on, and then continued to disobey and talk back, you were saying yes. You said yes, you wanted a paddling. And I believe I already offered to give you what you wanted tonight."

The exclamation point to his statement came in the form of the fifth stroke. Hard, fast, and unrelenting. She collapsed against the leather padding of the bench again when he released her waist.

The happy place slipped from her grasp, and she crashed back to where she lay in the dungeon. Her ass burned, her clit throbbed, and he squatted in front of her stroking her forehead while she returned to him.

"That part sucked, right?" he asked with a harsh tone, but his fingers never left her. The soothing sensation of his petting contradicted the sternness of his voice.

"Yeah," she answered, resting her cheek on the bench.

"Good." He patted her cheek.

CHAPTER 3

*T*ate took a long pull of his coffee and rubbed his eyes with the heels of his hands. He had a long day ahead of him, and he needed to get his mind right.

He shouldn't have stayed out so late, but making sure Sydney made it home safe and sound was paramount. She'd nearly spiked into subspace, and he would have been thrilled to send her there if only she'd been honest about what she wanted. But she'd held back, so he did the same.

Giving her an orgasm before inflicting her punishment had been slightly cruel, but he hadn't gotten this far in his career by not listening to his gut. Her getting those five with the wooden paddle after coming so damn hard really drove the punishment home. If he'd delivered them before she orgasmed, it would have just ramped up her arousal and the lesson would have been watered down.

What he couldn't figure out, or at least wasn't ready to admit, was why it was so important to him the lesson stuck? He'd played with other submissives who'd earned a chastisement for disobedience during a scene. And never once did he work so hard to see the lesson actually had a true impact. A little harder spanking to be sure she kept within the boundaries they had set, but nothing he expected to last longer than their playtime together. Yet, the spanking he'd given Sydney had a point, and he would be damned if he didn't make it plain for her to see it.

But nothing with Sydney made total sense to him. Not yet. He'd figure it all out, that he didn't doubt. But how much fight would she give him in the process? Why the hell didn't she give in to her own desires? She wasn't new to the scene. There was no reason for her to be shy, and she was too confident to be ashamed of wanting to be dominated, and punished. She hadn't been shy about telling him how she enjoyed the floggers but hated the wood implements, yet admitting she wanted something more than a light spanking seemed beyond her.

He'd figure her out later. He'd managed to get her phone number so he could check on her. He played casually, but he always made sure to call his bottoms to be sure they were doing okay a day or two later. Just because the scene was over, didn't mean it didn't stick with the players, and he wasn't going to allow a woman to go through a drop alone.

"You ready? The DA is in the meeting room already." John Trainer knocked on his doorjamb.

Tate downed the rest of his coffee and picked up the files from his desk. "Yeah. Let's get this over with. I don't understand why we even need this meeting. I'd think she would have had questions before you made your arrest." He shoved his arms into his jacket and ran his fingers through his hair. He'd barely woken up in time to shower before heading into the office.

Since Steinbeck collapsed at his desk a few days ago, the Stanley case had been dumped on Tate's shoulders. It was completed from what John, the second detective on the case, had told him. John had taken in a man for questioning and made the arrest. Michael Stanley should be standing before a judge having his bail set, not sitting around waiting for the DA to keep asking questions.

The buzz of the office remained unchanged from any other day. Phones rang, chatter went on around them as Tate followed John to the corner meeting room. Reserved for staff meetings, or ones such as this when the DA wanted to go over files that were pretty much self-explanatory.

Following John into the room, he closed the door behind him as his partner made the official greetings and introductions.

"Good morning, Ms. Richards. I'm Detective Trainer and this is Detective Tate, he's overseeing this case since Detective Steinbeck's heart attack."

Tate turned from the door with his hand already outstretched to shake the DA's hand and froze. Sydney stood before him. Pencil skirt, purple blouse too tight around her generous breasts, and her hair pinned up on her head in a tight bun.

He recovered faster than she did and gripped her hand, giving a gentle squeeze before releasing her. "Nice to see you," he said not moving to take a seat as John had.

"Y-yes." She nodded and cleared her throat. "Nathan Tate?" She clarified his name.

No one at the club used his first name, in fact no one close to him ever did at all. It was his father's name, one he'd prefer to forget.

"Just Tate is fine." He nodded toward the chairs situated around the oval desk. "Can we get you coffee or some water?"

Her eyes flickered from him to John and back. "No, thank you. I have another meeting right after this, and if Mr. Stanley is to be arraigned today we need to get started." And with that, she clamped shut her mouth. The soft submissive he held in his arms for almost an hour after their scene at the spanking bench was far from the iron maiden taking the chair across from where he and John were sitting.

"Sure thing, fire away." John leaned back in his chair, folding his hands behind his head, ready to go.

Sydney adjusted her seat and flipped open the files piled up in front of her. "Michael Stanley is in custody for the two murders that took place over a period of three days," she read off her notes detailing the case and the gruesome crime scenes.

"I know the case." Tate didn't need the recap, he'd seen the photos of the mangled bodies. Two women, both twenty-three years old, long hair, dark eyes, and curvy. The victims could have been fucking sisters. The case turned his stomach.

Sydney looked up at him, jaw clenched. "Right." She leaned back.

"So, what's the hold up, why haven't you filed the charges yet?" John asked.

"I have the filing ready to go, but I'm unsure you've arrested the right man." She picked up another piece of paper from her file. "I just—" she sighed. "Something doesn't feel right to me, and I was hoping you would be able to help. This suspect has an alibi for all three nights, that's going to make this case difficult."

"Flimsy alibi at best. An ex-girlfriend says he was with her, but they were at her place alone. No one saw them together," John pointed out.

"No one saw her without him that night either. She has no priors, not even a traffic ticket, and other than the drug charges, Michael Stanley has no history of criminal activity."

"So, because he got his ex-girlfriend to lie for him, this is going to fall apart?" John leaned forward, tensing. Too many cases were dropped that took them months to close.

Tate understood his tension, but also knew she had more to say.

"She didn't say that. Let her finish." Tate put a hand on John's shoulder. "Go on. What's the other question?"

"When he was arrested, he was on his way to work, right?"

"I stopped him on his way in to the factory he works at, yeah. Brought him in for questioning then made the arrest." Tate nodded.

"But there were no weapons on him or in his car. You searched his apartment and found nothing concrete that led you to those women?"

"His apartment is still being processed. The forensics team was there last night. We should start getting some information this afternoon. Besides, we had a tip," John explained fidgeting in his seat.

"Right. That's my point. If there hadn't been a tip called in, would you two have even looked at Mr. Stanley for the crimes? What made you pick him up for questioning in the first place? From what I could tell there isn't any evidence linking him to these murders."

It was Tate's turn to lean over the table, his hands flat. "The tip panned out, does that really matter?"

"It does." She focused on him, firm eyes, no hesitation in her at all. This was business. "He had no real connection to the girls. I spoke with the forensic team lead at the apartment this morning, and so far, they've found nothing that can put those girls in the suspect's apartment or even suggest he knew them."

Tate didn't have an answer for her. He'd only finished reading the files the day before, and although he had a few questions as well, he hadn't taken the time to talk with the forensics team. Sydney didn't waste time it seemed.

"What about his storage unit? They found a knife." John pointed out. "It fits the description of the knife used, according to the medical examiner. And there were tarps, too."

"Yes, both practically brand new. They are finishing the testing on those items, but I have the preliminary reports." She pulled out a piece of paper and slid it across the table for them. John ignored it, but Tate picked it up. He hadn't seen those results yet. "So far, no traces of blood, tissue, or even Mr. Stanley's prints. Those items were practically new."

Tate read over the report. She was right. Even if he had cleaned the knives, traces of blood would have been found.

"Detective Trainer, when you picked Mr. Stanley up for questioning, I was fine with that, having the tip called in and his alibi is a bit flimsy, but I don't think we have enough for a full arrest and we sure as hell don't have enough for a conviction," Sydney said, folding her hands on top of the files.

Tate slid the report back over to her.

John wasn't as calm as Tate, though. "Everything we had pointed to him. His car was seen driving away from the last crime scene. The witness saw the car drive down the alley just before he came across the women's bodies. True, Stanley didn't have a direct relationship with the women, but they all worked out at the same gym where he is a member."

"And did you cross-check to see if he used his membership at all during the times the women were there?" she questioned.

"Are you telling me you aren't going to file charges on him? You're going to let him go free so he can grab a third girl?" John asked, his hands fisted on the table.

"I'm telling you, I want to be sure I'm going to lock up the right asshole." Her temper started to peek through her resolve. She hadn't looked at Tate the entire meeting, only glancing in his direction but never actually making eye contact.

"He's the right guy."

"What's his motive?" she asked when John continued to press her.

"Rejection? Jealousy? Take a look at those women and then look at Stanley, a little out of his league." John looked over at Tate for some help, but Tate wasn't entirely sure where he stood at the moment.

"I'd like it better if those knives had more than just the right model number," Tate said. "Do the girls have a connection? Were they friends?"

John's shoulders slumped. "They both have memberships at the gym, but other than that I couldn't find a connection. I know he's the guy. When I showed him those photographs, I got no reaction from him. He just looked, blinked, and stared at me."

"Do you think we have enough to file charges? We might not have enough for a conviction right now, but if we don't file on him today we have to let him go." Tate watched Sydney as she considered his request.

"I can't file charges on someone because your partner has a hunch." She looked back at John.

"You didn't see how he looked at those photographs," John said with a hint of desperation.

She sighed. "Fine. I'll file them, but maybe the judge will kick it. If you don't have more evidence, a solid case soon, I'm dropping the charges. I won't be responsible for putting an innocent man behind bars." The tiny shake to her voice when she made her statement stuck out to Tate. There was more at stake for her than just finding the right killer.

"And if he's guilty?" John's sour tone did not help lighten the tension building in the small conference room.

"If he's the guy, I'll nail his balls to the bench." Not even a twitch of her cheek, just straight-laced confidence. As though Tate needed yet another reason to find the woman attractive.

"Then we'll get the evidence and make the case solid," Tate promised, not giving John a second thought.

Sydney smiled. "Thank you. That would definitely help." She still hadn't looked directly at him, and now she busied herself with cleaning up the files and shoving them into her bag.

John huffed, but stood up from the table. "We'll call you when we have something that'll make you happy." He gave Tate an exasperated look and marched out of the room, letting the door slam behind him.

Tate didn't move from his chair, he just continued to watch her putting the files in order and sliding them into her briefcase while trying to pretend she didn't feel his presence in the room.

* * *

HIS EYES WERE STILL on her. She could feel them burrowing into her as she repacked her files. Her nerves were already frayed enough just from seeing him walk into the room with Detective Trainer, having him stare her down now when she was trying to grasp everything without losing her composure was almost too much.

Their time at the club the night before hadn't faded into a dull memory yet, and at the moment, she needed to keep her focus on the case. She'd done a damn good job, she thought, of keeping herself in control even with being thrown off by his presence. Keeping her attention on the evidence and the suspect in custody was the only way to keep herself from delving into the delicious memory of being under his command.

The meeting could have gone better, but at least she got what she wanted, more digging. She would go all in on the case, nail the asshole's balls to the floor if he was guilty, but she wasn't for nailing the nearest bad guy just because he was there.

At least Tate understood, even if his partner didn't.

"I didn't realize you were a district attorney." Tate finally spoke once the last latch of her briefcase snapped closed.

"I'm not. Not yet. Right now, I'm still an assistant DA." She grabbed the handle of her case and took a deep breath. "You didn't tell me you were a detective, either."

"Didn't really come up in conversation." He grinned. The little crease on the right side of his mouth surfaced with his grin, and she felt her stomach start to knot up again. It was hard enough trying to forget all about him that morning without having to actually run into him. Now it looked like she'd be working right alongside him.

"Well, thank you for being so cooperative, and, well, discrete."

His chair scraped along the linoleum flooring, and he rounded the table, coming to stand at her side within a few strides. "Look at me," he ordered. That same dark voice as the night before. But they weren't at Black Light. And she wasn't his to order about.

"We're at work," she reminded him, but found herself tilting her head back to look up at him regardless.

He looked down at her with hard eyes, his jaw set. "Yes. And it looks like we might be working together on this case, so while we are working things stay strictly professional. But when we are alone, and not working the case, things are different. Yes?"

He hadn't shaved that morning. Whiskers covered his jaw, and he looked as tired as she felt. Maybe he hadn't slept well either.

"Of course, well, I mean when we are at work. There really is no reason for us to be together outside of this case, so—" She cleared her throat, letting the last of her words die away.

His left eyebrow arched, a pointed peak letting her know how much he disliked her statement. "I don't think that's true."

"I really do have another meeting to get to, Detective Tate." She put her hand out, gesturing for a final handshake before she left. She couldn't have that conversation, didn't want to have it. He was everything she couldn't allow to sneak into her life. The crush she'd been harboring since seeing him play at Black Light months ago needed to stay in her fantasies. Because dark fantasies like hers didn't come true.

He took her hand, his thumb caressing her palm. "Fine. Fair enough. Tell me how you feel this morning, then. About last night."

Her eyes shot up to his. She tried to get her hand back, but he gripped harder. To anyone outside the room it would look like they were just talking.

"I just said we aren't going to discuss those things while I'm working." She managed to keep her voice down by grinding her teeth together.

"You have two choices then, Sydney. One, you answer my question now, or two, you answer them tonight at my place."

"Your place?" she asked. She needed to breathe, somewhere away from the intoxicating scent of him. Since when did soap become an aphrodisiac?

"Yes. I have your number, I'll text the address." He released her hand.

"I- I can't."

"Can't or won't? What are you so afraid of? Me? Or you?"

She took a step back, not willing to crane her neck to look at him anymore. Afraid of herself? What a stupid suggestion. Almost laughable.

Her phone dinged from her purse. She would barely make it back to her office in time if she left right then. She didn't have time to argue with him.

"Fine. Text me. And then we can just be professionals." She yanked her briefcase from the table and slipped around him, throwing the door of the room open and nearly stomping out. She kept her footing at an even pace, and avoided all the stares she could feel burning into her back as she made her way through the precinct.

She'd meet him at his apartment, answer his questions, assure him she was fine and then she'd leave.

No problem.

* * *

No detective she'd ever met lived in such a place. He was obviously over paid.

Sydney stepped onto the elevator, admiring the marble flooring of the lobby as the doors slid closed. The newest construction on the block it would appear, and no way a detective's salary could be paying for the high-class condominium right off the river.

When she stepped off the elevator she expected to find a hallway and a few different doors. What she actually encountered was a small foyer and a single door with a doorbell and security keypad.

She pressed the bell and waited for a butler dressed in fine livery to open the door.

"Sydney. Hi." Tate stood in the open doorway, holding the door in one hand and leaning on the frame with the other, a sly grin on his face.

"Hey." She couldn't help the smile she returned, the man looked too happy for her to be so sulky. But she would have to try harder. She needed to get out of the evening unscathed.

"Come in." He ushered her in, grabbing her coat and purse and depositing them in a closet nearby. She stood slack jawed looking around the open floor plan of the most appealing home she'd even been inside. Although the building reeked of wealth and power, his condo, which apparently took up the entire floor, was nothing but a relaxing Zen-like area.

"Wow." She spun around, taking in the warm colors and comfortable decor. "This place is beautiful." Her cheeks heated when she looked back up at him, surprise lingering in his eyes.

"You like it? Most woman find it too man-caveish."

"Man cave?" She laughed and waved a hand, walking further into the condo toward the living area where two large, over-stuffed couches faced an enormous flat screen television. "Is that one of those curved TVs?" She walked around the couch and took a look, admiring the technology.

"Yeah, makes the movies look more realistic—at least that's what the sales guy said."

"Not sports? Usually guys with TVs like this are into sports." She walked back around the TV and stood center of the room.

"I'm not really into them. Not much time to keep up with work and all that." His hands were shoved into his front pockets, making his already broad shoulders appear larger.

The pain in her shoulders from the tension she'd been harboring eased off. So easily, just within moments of being in his presence, she found herself relaxed, like visiting an old friend. But he wasn't an old friend. As handsome and tempting as he was, she needed to remember to keep things professional between them. She straightened her stance. "Yeah. Work."

"Dinner's almost done. Can I get you some wine or water or something?"

"Dinner?" She became aware of the scent of roast beef in the air. Of course, he would make dinner. He'd asked her over after work, normal people ate dinner after work. "No, thanks. I mean, it smells great, but I need to get home. So, can we just get on with this?" She fought the urge to put her hands on her hips and instead put her most serious expression forward.

Tate stared at her in silence, a storm brewed before her, but she wasn't sure what to do about it. He obviously went to some length to prepare a meal for them. His expectations were more than just a quick Q&A session, but she wasn't sure she'd get out of that conversation in one piece. She'd seen him play, had seen him with his subs even when they weren't strapped to a bench bare-assed. He'd never given her any reason to believe he would let her get away with a quick *I'm fine* and let her out the door.

It would be easy to fall onto the awfully comfy looking couch and just talk with him all night. The roulette game had proven to her how at ease he could put her when they were talking, but it had also shown her he could see through her, leaving her completely exposed to him without much ammunition to stop it. Having dinner with him would only make the transparency, well, more transparent.

"Get on with it?" he asked. His dark gaze made the couch between them shrink about three sizes.

"You said you wanted to be sure I'm okay. I don't know why you couldn't just call or maybe text, email even." She waved a hand through the air. Even she wasn't buying her fake indifference, no way he'd buy it. Amazing how quickly insecurities can make an intelligent woman drop a few IQ points.

The condo was too inviting, too comforting. She needed to get the hell out of there before anything that shouldn't happen did.

"Are you? Okay?"

"Yes. I'm fine." She nodded and let out an exaggerated sigh. How could she be fine? The evening before had unsettled something inside of her. As though all the perfectly placed bricks she'd used to build her little wall around her had shifted, leaving it ready to topple with the next slight breeze. The spanking had been in tune with everything she'd ever wanted in a play session. He didn't go easy, and he would have taken her much further if she hadn't been so damn stubborn.

He didn't cave to her taunt, and that alone stroked her submissive side. The punishment, although only a few strikes of the paddle, had left her regretting not following his orders about her thong. It would be dangerous to get too close to him, because he'd already gotten too close to her.

He didn't move an inch closer to her, but she could feel the heat rolling off his body just the same. It didn't help matters that he looked so damn skeptical.

"I think there's more to that answer." At least his tone remained causal, even if his body tensed.

How could she manage to hide her real feelings with him staring at her so intently? Averting her gaze, she noted a poster hanging on the wall behind him. Star Trek the Next Generation's Wesley Crusher, and it was signed! Wil Wheaton's signature sprawled out across the bottom left hand corner. And beside the poster were several pieces of memorabilia, that even her untrained eye could see were not things a detective on the D.C. force could afford.

"Sydney." Tate snapped her attention back to him.

"Where'd you get those things?" She jerked her finger at the poster and other items. He followed her outstretched hand. "And this condo? No detective could afford this part of town let alone the entire floor in a new high rise!" *Way to distract him, Syd. Insult and distract. Clever much?*

Tate still made no move toward her. His lids narrowed just a fraction, just enough to put a wrinkle around the edges of his eyes. "Sydney."

"No. You know what? No. I don't need to know. I'm pretty sure I have a good idea of what's going on. And I want nothing to do with a corrupt cop." Maybe if he was busy defending himself he wouldn't notice her own unease about talking through their scene of the previous evening.

"Corrupt? What?" He sounded surprised at her accusation. But didn't most criminals? "You think I have money because I'm on some scumbag's payroll?" No more surprise, just pure offense steeped with anger.

"Uh." She could read reactions pretty well, which helped when she was trying a case, and his current glare had nothing to do with being found out and everything to do with not liking being accused.

"You know, plenty of cops take on extra shifts. Work doubles whenever they can for extra cash or to earn more vacation time. It's amazing how quickly money compounds when invested well."

"Invested?" Could her entire shoe fit in her mouth, or just up to her heel?

"Invested." He nodded with dark eyes, but still he hadn't moved a muscle. "A few shares in a restaurant, more at a nightclub and a few sprinkled other places around town. Surprised a cop could actually put his money to work for him?"

"No." She shook her head. She really wasn't surprised. Tate never came across as anything other than perfectly put together and smart. Of course, he would take his extra earnings and make them work for him.

"I'll just grab my stuff and go." Her stomach tensed. Nothing was going the way she'd planned. Though she had no right to think he wouldn't have been ready for a normal evening. Normal dinner, normal conversation. She had no right, but her fear of exposing something she wasn't ready to unleash kept her from using the intelligence she possessed and used quite well every other minute of the day.

Accusing him of being on the take, because she couldn't sort out how the hell she felt about their play session? Real mature!

It shouldn't be so damn hard to have conflicting feelings. She should be able to sort them out on her own. Hadn't her mother raised her to deal with these things on her own? To sort it all out because no one was coming to untangle her mess for her.

He didn't say a word when she passed him, but she could feel the heat of his glare on her, burning into her back. Her shoes made the faintest sound as she walked to the front door. She almost made it to the closet where she'd seen him stash her stuff before she heard his command.

"Not another step."

CHAPTER 4

$\mathcal{H}$ e didn't expect her to listen. Hand to heaven, he was positive she was going to leave her purse behind and bolt for the elevator. So, when she froze in front of the closet and slowly turned back to him, he wasn't fully prepared.

Taking a moment to get his irritation under control, he refocused his concentration on her. It seemed obvious to him she was nervous. Maybe she had a bad history with men in general, or she'd seen some really bad shit as a prosecutor and simply assumed everyone had a bad angle to them. None of that justified her accusations, but it might explain how easy she jumped to all the wrong conclusions.

"Sydney, we aren't done talking," he said.

She rolled her head back and let loose a heavy sigh. "Tate, what happened at the club won't happen again. Obviously, we aren't matched well. So, it's probably better we just leave things professional. We'll get this case all done with, and then we'll go about our merry ways."

Did she even know how much her voice shook when she pushed him? She'd done the same thing the night of Roulette. She'd wanted a harder spanking than he'd given her when they first sat down at their table. Not knowing her well enough, he'd only given her a few swats to her skirt-covered ass before the scenes for the evening began playing out around them. But she didn't ask for more or for harder, she'd just started in with her bratting.

"Sydney, I'm asking you to have dinner with me. I'm not asking you to wear my collar or crawl naked through my house, or suck my cock while I eat." Though all of those thoughts had serious merit in his book. "Are you so afraid of me that you can't even do that?"

She huffed, a forced laugh that didn't match the apprehension in her eyes. "Afraid of you? No."

"Good, then. Like I said, dinner's ready. Do you want a glass of wine or water?"

Her fingers wiggled at her sides, the tension in her shoulders hadn't let up yet. Whatever battle raged inside that beautiful head of hers wasn't going to be easily won.

"You have a habit of jumping to conclusions, don't you? And wrong ones, from what I've seen so far." He tried a new tactic when she still hadn't moved or responded. "At the game, I heard you telling your friend's partner that I said you weren't my type, that I couldn't handle you. But that's not what I said."

"Yes, it is." Her eyes widened.

He shrugged and turned his back to her, sauntering toward the kitchen. Just as he hoped, she followed him, her flats clipping along the tile until she walked over the carpeting of the living room to get to the kitchen.

"That is what you said," she told him with more heat, as he pulled the roast out of the oven. Perfectly cooked, just like his mom's.

"No. It's not." He went about grabbing plates and silverware, placing them on the counter-top while he finished draining the potatoes.

"Whatever. Maybe you're too old, your memory's fading." She

leaned against the kitchen island and crossed her arms over her chest. Sulking, but at least present.

He laughed and shook his head. "Brats tend to switch to rudeness when all their bratting gets them is ignored." He pointed a finger in the air and moved down the length of his cabinets to find the potato smasher.

"I'm not a brat!" she yelled at him, stomping her right foot and slamming her hand on the countertop.

He paused in his movements and turned back to her, tilting his head and staring at her. It only took a moment for the impact of her actions to show on her cheeks. Her creamy white skin quickly blushed.

"You aren't a good one, no. You use bratting because you don't know how to ask for what you want. And when bratting doesn't work, you get pissy, and when pissy doesn't work, you storm off." He went back to mashing the potatoes.

"You told me I wasn't your type." She looked physically pained by holding back the stomping of her foot.

He pushed the pot of mashed potatoes further back on the stove and made sure all the burners were off before stepping over to her.

He didn't touch her. He didn't need to. When he placed his left hand on the island and leaned over her, she swallowed hard, her eyes wide. He had her attention.

"I said I don't usually go for the bratty type. I said brats don't usually handle my rules well."

She tilted her head back slightly, her lips parted, but she remained silent.

"I never once said you weren't my type. I never once said I couldn't handle you— because I can handle you just fine, Sydney. I'm just not sure you're ready to be handled."

She looked ready to slap him, but remained stoic. Good start. He suspected it had either been a long time since someone had seen through her smoke screen, or maybe no one had bothered in the past.

"I'm not going to force you or chase you. If you'd rather walk out of here and go home, I'll respect that. We'll stay completely professional. Detective and prosecutor." He wouldn't chase her, but he'd want to. He would have to talk himself out of running after her, but he could manage it. If he had to.

"And if I stay?" she asked after several heartbeats of silence.

His chest lightened, and his breath came easier. Fighting back the knowing grin, he gave her a little space. "If you stay, we have dinner. We talk. We get to know each other."

She worried at her lower lip while her fingers drummed on the counter. "I, okay." Dropping her hand from the counter she stood straight and gave him a curt nod.

"Good." He winked at her and turned back to plating their dishes. "C'mon." He gestured for her to follow him as he carried the plates to the dining table. He'd gotten her to the dinner table, no small feat. Did she even realize how much energy she wasted fighting herself on getting what she wanted? They could have been past the roast and onto dessert by the time she finally accepted having dinner with him was exactly what she wanted, and what she really had come over for. Blowing him off would have answered his question of whether there was anything between them other than a few nights of chemistry. But she hadn't.

Once they were settled, she picked up her fork and knife, pausing over the roast. "I'm sorry about what I said." She pointed toward the living room with her fork.

"I'm sure you've seen plenty of cops who were on someone's payroll, or at least easily bribed," he conceded.

She shifted in her seat and shoved a forkful of roast into her mouth.

"Yes, I've seen things like that, and not all just while I've been a prosecutor. I don't think cops who do that—who start working for the assholes of the city—can understand what it does to the innocent families they hurt. Framing men for things they didn't do, ripping fathers away from their families." She shook her head and blinked a few times. "Corruption pisses me off," she said and dove back into her food.

"Not my favorite thing either." He smiled at her, bringing his glass of water to his lips. Her cheeks tinted pink, and she shifted her seat again.

"Me being the prosecutor on your case doesn't bother you?"

He swallowed some potatoes and shrugged. "Why would that bother me? We're on the same side."

"Well, technically, yes, but I could decide not to prosecute this guy. I could decide to take a deal you don't like. I've had other detectives get more than a little irritated by my calls in the past."

She grabbed a small piece of beef from the fork with her teeth.

"Yes, you could do any of those things. It's your job to do them." He gulped down more of his water. "Are you asking if that changes the dynamic of this?" He waggled a finger between them.

"Yeah. I mean, if you're big dom guy at home, won't not being in control at the office be a problem?"

He put his fork down and studied her for a minute. The idea of their jobs being an issue hadn't occurred to him.

"I enjoy being in control in a relationship with a woman, a consenting woman, and only in regards to her personal safety and our personal lives. When it comes to work, I keep my hands off. I don't need to be in control of every situation. So, no, I don't think it's going to be a problem."

"And if someone else thinks it is?"

"Then we'll deal with it."

She took a deep breath. "Like how?"

He shot her a smile. "We'll worry about that if it happens."

She fiddled with her fork for a long moment. "Okay, I think I can do that."

Talking with her over a meal came easy. No awkward silences

to wade through. They sat at the table long after the uneaten food on their plates got cold, just talking and laughing. The woman had snark and wit unlike he'd come across before. Nothing forced, she just naturally had a way of lightening the room with her banter.

"Let me help you clean up." She picked up her plate and reached across for his. He handed it to her with a thank you and went about grabbing the empty water glasses. She rinsed off the plates and tucked them in his dishwasher. "I absolutely love this place," she said as she walked back into the living room after the dishwasher had started up.

He watched her walking around the room, fingering the spines of the books he had piled here and there.

"A reader?" she asked with a grin.

"My mom taught high school English, reading was more of a requirement than chores when I was growing up."

"Ahh, a mommy's boy?" She teased him, but he wasn't taking the bait.

"Nah, I left that to my little brother. Followed in her footsteps and everything." He rounded the couch and came to stand close to her. "But I don't want to talk about my mom and brother." He lightly touched her arm, feeling the soft cotton of her shirt, beneath it her soft skin went untouched.

"Oh? Did you want to chat about the weather? Unseasonably warm? Or cold?" The corner of her mouth turned up, while her eyes narrowed.

"I want to talk about last night." He snagged her elbow and brought her to the couch, dragging her to sit on his lap.

She exaggerated her oomph and twisted until she could stare at him. He raised his eyebrow in response, and tapped his finger against her forehead. "Ever heard the phrase *I believe the lady doth protest too much?*"

He rubbed away her frown and waited until she softened her expression.

"Fine, what about last night? It was fine. We talked after,

remember?" She squirmed in his lap, but he managed to still her with an arm draped over her legs.

"Yes, I remember. I remember I gave in and let you get away with wanting to wait to talk until later. Well, it's later." He tapped her thigh with his finger. "How is your butt?" He patted her rump with his left hand.

"My butt is fine." Another soft pink hue touched her cheeks.

"Any marks?" He managed to keep his hands on the outside of her pants, but if she continued her wiggling he couldn't promise such good behavior in the very near future.

"Nope." She shook her head and squirmed until she straddled his waist, flattening her hands on his chest. "Ass of steel this one." She wiggled her backside against his thighs.

"Sydney, do you want a spanking?"

As he suspected she pulled back, her face bright crimson.

"Just because I'm on your lap? You put me here."

"No, because you're being sarcastic and not taking this seriously."

"You asked if my butt was okay. It's okay." She nodded and slipped off his lap, staying on the couch but backing away from him. "Did you want to check yourself?" She smirked. "Is that it? You want a way into my pants without having to work for it?"

Sydney didn't take the easy road. But that was fine, he hadn't had an adventure in a while.

* * *

TATE STARED at her for a long minute. Probably more like seconds, but when a man with a serious resting face like his turns even more serious, it can feel as though time obeys only him.

"I hadn't planned on getting in your pants tonight, but if that's what you want, far be it from me not give it to you." He left her on the couch and took a seat in the armchair in the far corner of the room. "Stand up and take off your pants and your panties. Keep your shirt on, not interested in those tits just yet."

"I didn't mean to get your boxers in a bunch," she insisted without moving from the couch. She had a real knack at souring the mood. When would she learn to just let the river flow without throwing so many damn boulders in the way?

"Sydney. Here's my number one rule, pay attention now. I don't want you telling me later you didn't understand. Here it is: I tell you what to do, you do it."

She'd heard that line before. Standard dom rule. Not many would actually back it up, though. Most would give up before she could get what she wanted. But a dark cloud shadowed Tate's expression. Maybe he could handle her.

"If I have to repeat myself things get worse for you." His fingers drummed on the arm of the chair, but his feet remained planted, and he made no move to make a grab for her.

She gave a little sigh, and shoved off the couch. Keeping her gaze locked with his, she fumbled through unbuttoning and unzipping her jeans. He didn't watch her hands as they worked the skinny jeans off, but instead he remained fixated on her face. A few seconds in, and she found holding his stare difficult. As though he cut through her, trying to see below the surface.

Nothing worth seeing there, big boy.

Once she was bared, she kicked her panties and jeans to the side and folded her hands in front of herself. He still hadn't looked at her body. The inattention to her curves was more unnerving than if he had fully inspected her. Damn him for knowing how to get under her skin.

"Was that it?" She rolled her shoulders back and thrust her chin. "Just wanted to see me strip?"

The right side of his mouth cocked upward, and his chest puffed out in a short burst of a huff. "The brattier you get the more I understand." He pointed to the spot on the floor before him. "Come stand here."

She rolled her eyes and moved into position. "I'm not a brat."

He shook his head at her answer. "Now, put your hands behind your back." He leaned back in his chair, still making no move to touch her.

Tilting her head to the side, she folded her arms behind her. They weren't getting anywhere, and his huffing and puffing wasn't going to make her scared. She knew this routine. Make her feel vulnerable, give her a spanking to awaken her libido, only to leave her hanging, and then send her on her way. Tate was turning out to be more typical than she had already feared.

His lips formed a full smile, and he arranged himself in his chair, getting more comfortable. "You think you'll be getting a little spanking? Something to show you who's boss around here?"

"That is the normal course of events for these sorts of things, right?" She dug her nails into her forearms. A little bite of pain to keep herself awake.

"And why would I spank you? Because you got a little snarky? Bordered on disrespect when I'm trying to take care of you after our scene last night? Maybe because of the offensive accusations you threw at me earlier?" He still hadn't touched her. That fact shouldn't have gripped her so damn hard. *And why would he? Every step he takes toward you, you throw a tantrum. For once don't be your own enemy!*

"If that's what you think, sure. You're the top here, right?" *Ugh! Get a grip, Sydney!*

"Top." His lips screwed up into a frown and nodded. "Do you think there's a difference between a top and a dominant?"

"I'm sure there are a million chat rooms that can answer that question better than me."

"There are, you're right. I'm asking for your opinion. What's the difference?"

The insecure part of her brain finally shut up to let her articulate-self show up to the party. "To me, a top is the guy I'm playing with, things end after the scene. A dominant is long term, like after the scene stops, he's still in charge."

He nodded, approval spreading across his features. "So, a dominant is someone you have a relationship with?"

"Yes, but that's just my definition. Like I said, there's a ton of chatrooms where the opinions vary."

He ignored her lengthy justification. "So, I'm just a top?"

"You were last night," she shot at him, the twenty questions weren't getting them anywhere.

He let out his apparent exasperation. "And what do you want? Do you want a top or do you want a dominant?"

She took a small step back. Tiny really, but enough to realize what she'd done. It was the question, she assured herself, not the dark tone in which he asked it that made her hesitate. No one had ever asked that question before.

The air grew heavy between them. He waited for his answer, and she tried to come up with one her mouth would be willing to speak. Don't ask and you won't get rejected. It really was simple. Didn't he know that rule?

Still not looking at her bared sex, his shoulders dropped a bit, and his eyes moved to her shoulders. "Turn around."

Sydney faced away from him and jumped slightly when his fingertips touched her bare ass. He wasn't stroking her or rubbing in anyway sexual, but the feathery touch still sent her nerve endings into over drive.

"You have a small bruise here." He poked at the offensive mark. She'd seen it after getting out of the shower that morning, but it was too small to mention.

"From the paddle, no doubt." She bit her lip to keep from saying anything else. The bite of the wood would have been exhilarating if he hadn't just given her a mind-blowing orgasm. Everything tingled after an orgasm, and what normally would be a delightful pain was just pain in those moments.

"Probably. It's small and should fade in a day or so. Does it hurt?" He actually sounded concerned.

"No. Ow! Except when you do that!" She looked over her shoulder to glare at him for poking the tender area. He didn't even have the courtesy to look remorseful.

"Everything looks fine. You can get dressed." He patted her hip and stood, shimmying around her and still not touching her.

What the hell was wrong with him? She was half naked and standing in his living room.

"Dressed?" She had to have heard him wrong.

"Yeah." He scooped up her jeans and panties and held them out to her.

She unraveled her arms from behind her and took the pile.

"I'm going to make coffee. You want some?"

"No." She shook her head and went about dressing as fast as she could. He obviously had found her wanting, and she wanted to get the hell out of his condo.

After buttoning her jeans she looked up. He hadn't left the room. He just stood there watching her. It wasn't fair to be pissed at a man she found so attractive. It wasn't fair that she wasn't good enough for him. It was her damn mouth. Couldn't she just leave off her protective armor of obnoxiousness just once?

"It's late." She excused herself and headed to the closet to retrieve her coat and purse.

Her coat was removed from her hands as soon as she took it from the hanger. She whipped around, ready to argue with him, but found him holding it out for her to put her arms through the sleeves. Some of the anger dissipated, but the humiliation burned just as hot.

He'd flat out rejected her, and she hadn't even divulged her true desires.

She kept her eyes away from him as she slid her arms into her coat and let him pull it up for her, straightening out the collar as he did.

"I'm going to be at Black Light on Saturday," he said and turned her around to face him.

He cupped her chin and pulled her face upward, until she had no choice but to look at him again. It shouldn't hurt to look at something so beautiful, but the knot in her chest was there all the same.

"You have until then to decide if you want a top or a dom. Personally, I'm looking for something that lasts longer than a scene at the club. You don't want to tell me what you want, but I'm not going to push. I have a few suspicions as to why that is, but we'll work it all out." His thumb ran along her jaw. "But first you have to tell me how this is going to go. And be prepared, Sydney, because if you want a dom, you'll have me—all of me. And I'm not all that easy going. I will make you explore those parts you keep hiding with your brattiness. I will make you push those comfort zones. But I will be there to hold you through it all. I won't let you do it alone, and I won't let you fall."

She heard every word he said, which was a feat of its own considering the hammering of her heart in her chest. Being told almost every line out there to date, this one caught her off guard.

"Those are some big words." She tried to smile, to downplay the seriousness of his tone, but it didn't work. His eyes remained as stern as before.

"Saturday." He released her chin and reached around her to grab her purse, handing it to her before opening the front door.

She didn't give him another look, and the elevator gods were on her side. As soon as she pressed the button the doors slid open.

Saturday. Barely enough time.

She gave a little wave as the doors closed, and once they were shut, she leaned against the wall of the elevator touching her chin where he'd cupped it.

CHAPTER 5

*T*ate held up another medical examiner report, trying to decipher the terms and numbers. He'd seen less confusing data when he read through his father's polling reports —and those numbers were meant to confuse and disillusion.

"Any luck with that bullshit?" John walked into his office carrying a cup of coffee and his usual three o'clock sandwich.

Tate hadn't planned on coming into the office on a Saturday. They were still waiting for reports from the forensics teams and the coroner reports, so they were at a bit of a standstill.

But he needed a distraction. Something to take his mind off the complete fool he'd made of himself with Sydney. Giving her a chance to walk away had been stupid. She wasn't ready to voice her desires, that much was as plain to see as the adorable birthmark situated directly under her right earlobe.

"No." He tossed the report back in the open file sitting on his desk. "I can see where there's questions though. There are some pretty large holes in the case." He scratched his chest. "I think we should go over everything again. Comb through the circumstantial shit and see if we can make it more solid. Start at the beginning."

48

"The case is solid enough. That DA just needs to do her job." John took a long sip of his coffee.

"It's our job to get the evidence and arrest the right guy. It's her job to put the asshole away. If we don't do our job, she can't do hers." If it had been any other DA, he might have agreed with John, or at the least not been so twisted up about making sure the case was solid.

Not that Sydney needed his help. Her job was one area where she needed no assistance. From what he'd found out about her, she was like a wild animal when it came to trying her cases. She won more than she lost, and was well known for being passionate about putting the guilty away. Her need to be sure Stanley was the real killer showed how true the stories were. If she felt the arrested man wasn't the guy, she didn't try the case until either she was sure or the detectives were able to convince her.

As a result, some detectives hated working with her on a case, and John didn't hide the fact he was one of them.

"We gave her a good case. She's just being a pain in the ass." He leaned over Tate's desk and flipped the file closed. "Forget this for now. I have a new case, a girl out in Logan Circle."

"Related?"

"Not that I see. I'm heading out to the crime scene now."

"You need company?" Tate didn't need another case to follow, especially on his day off, but it would be hours before he would step into Black Light, and he needed to keep himself busy.

"Nah, should be pretty easy. Drugs, crazy ex-boyfriend." He tapped a finger on the Stanley file. "This one should be easy." With that, he bit into his sandwich, a piece of lettuce falling onto the standard issue, gray, metal desk, and left the office. Tate followed him with his eyes until he was back in his own office and shut the door.

If the case had been as solid as John led on, Chief Xander wouldn't have put him on it when Steinbeck had gone on disability leave.

Dragging his hand through his hair, he closed his eyes. Sydney, bent over that spanking bench with her perfectly round ass upturned, slightly red from the hand spanking invaded his mind.

Growling, he pushed back from his desk. He had to get that woman out of his mind, or he was going to lose it. If she didn't show up at Black Light there wouldn't be anything else he could do. The game would be forfeit.

"Hey, did you want to see me?" Jason, the forensic guru, came into his office.

"Yes!" Tate jumped at the chance to get back into work. "I can't read these reports. I need you to translate them for me. And when am I going to get finalized reports on Stanley's apartment and the storage unit?"

* * *

SYDNEY SAT in the back of Dane's sedan, tapping her feet on the floorboard of the car. Riley twisted around as much as she could without Dane giving her the evil eye, but Sydney only half listened to her anyway.

"Are you sure about this?" Riley asked.

Riley had been her best friend since she could remember. It had been accompanying her to the Roulette game on Valentine's Day at Black Light that led Sydney to sharing a table with Tate.

"I'd be a hell of a lot surer if *he* weren't going to be there." Sydney gave a pointed look to the back of Dane's head. She knew Dane well enough, had known him much better years and years ago, when he'd dated Riley the first time. But even with the passage of time, he could still be more protective than she needed. Her being their third wheel probably put him in that mindset, though. As far as Dane would see it, her being alone at Black Light meant he would be responsible for her. It didn't matter how many times she reminded him he was dating Riley, not her, he still took it upon himself to watch out for her.

Dane and Riley had really been giving their reconnection the full attention it deserved. And while Sydney was glad her two friends had reconnected, having him at the club when she met up with Tate was not what she wanted or needed.

"We'll be on the other side of the club. I promise." Dane caught her eye in the rearview mirror. "Keep him away from the medical play area, and you'll be fine."

"Medical play?" Riley turned to him. "You never said anything about that."

Dane lifted one hand from the steering wheel and patted her thigh. "Relax. We'll talk it all out before we start. And before the end of it, you'll be begging me to get to it. Now turn around."

Sydney sat back in her seat twiddling her fingers in her lap. What if Tate wasn't there? What if he'd thought it over and decided she *was* too much trouble? That's what most of the doms she got involved with did. Too much of a bother, and they walked. Maybe it would be better just to stick to play partners. Spanking partners didn't demand as much raw honesty as Tate would.

If he was even there.

"Don't worry, he'll be there." Riley, the mind reader, assured her. "It's going to be fine. You've had this man under your skin since the roulette game. It's about time you guys got together."

"He has not been under my skin."

Dane laughed as he pulled the car into a parking spot. "Even I can see how much you like him, Syd. Just take the chance. Worst that happens is it doesn't work out, right?"

Once the car shifted into park, she pushed open her door. "No, the worst that can happen is I fall totally in love with him and *then* it doesn't work out."

"You want me to talk him?" Riley asked, hooking her arm through Sydney's as they made their way to the psychic shop and toward the hidden entryway into Black Light. The chill of winter still lingered in the air, never mind it was already March and spring should be arriving.

"What? Are we in middle school again?" Sydney gave her an exasperated laugh, but hugged her arm tighter. "I'll be fine. I just need to get my head out of my ass."

Dane's gloved hand opened the door to the psychic shop and held it for them as they walked through. "Generally, it's best to keep your head out of your ass all the time."

Sydney rolled her eyes at Riley. "Still as unfunny as ever."

Riley laughed, but hushed herself quickly when they approached Luis. As bouncers went, he had the right look. All muscle with a well-placed scar on his cheek. If anyone ever found it odd to find him standing at the back of the shop, they'd think twice before commenting on it.

Sydney released Riley into Dane's care at the main check-in. Danny opened the lockers for them and kept up a casual conversation with one of the other DMs she didn't recognize. Sydney folded her coat and placed it, along with her purse and cell phone, into the locker before pushing it closed.

"We're going in. You sure you're okay?" Riley asked.

"I'm fine. It's just a guy." Who could tear her heart in shreds before the night was over, but still just a guy. Deep breath in, hold, breathe out.

Riley raised an eyebrow and shook her head. "Yeah. So was Dane." With that, she squeezed her arm and went to Dane who waited for her at the door.

Taking a minute, Sydney took in a few more breaths, and smoothed her hands over the dark purple dress she'd worn. Black was her color, especially given the deep brown coloring of her hair, but she'd bought the flirty number six months ago, and hadn't taken it out of the closet. Hopefully, it wouldn't be the only bold move she was willing to make for the evening.

"Sydney?" Danny called her over with a wave of his hand. "I have a note here for you." He reached into his back pocket and retrieved a folded piece of paper.

"Thanks." She took the note and stepped back to read it, her stomach twisting as she worked the paper open.

I've left a box in the costume room for you. If you've come as my submissive, change into what I've left and wait for me there. If you've come as a play partner, meet me in the bar area.

She let out her breath in a long whoosh. He hadn't stood her up. He was here. And he was leaving all the cards on the table for her to deal.

"Sydney, you going in?" Danny asked when a few more couples had come through the door, bringing cool air of outside with them.

"Yeah. Don't rush me," she muttered. "Making a choice here." She pressed herself against the counter, but scooted over to allow the other members to have their cards scanned and enter the dungeon.

Danny laughed. "I'd say you already made your choice. Not sure what Tate put in that note, but I do know relief when I see it."

She couldn't argue with that. If she was going to give this a real chance, she needed to put all her cards on the table. When she talked with Tate, she'd let him know everything. Tell him all of it, and if he didn't run for the hills and think her too hardcore, she'd know it was the right thing to do.

"Okay, let me in." She nodded and handed him her card. She'd spent so much time at the club, illuminating the membership card with his black light was mere formality, but still needed to be done. It was that focus on safety and keeping the members of the club anonymous that gave her the comfort level she needed to delve into her fantasies.

Stepping into Black Light awakened her senses. She inhaled and smiled. Leather and sex. Nothing smelled better.

The club was already busy for the evening. Couples played throughout the darkened dungeon. The St. Andrew's crosses were illuminated, and she could see from where she stood near the entrance door a woman being escorted onto the circular platform. She swallowed hard and took another calming breath.

The main stage was dark, unless there was going to be a demonstration it probably wouldn't be used tonight.

She glanced toward the bar, but the already crowded club blocked her from seeing if Tate was watching her or not. The tingling in her body suggested his eyes were on her, but she couldn't get confirmation.

Get it together, Sydney!

Sydney moved through the room holding her head up and trying her best to keep her eyes up and not search for him. She didn't need to seem desperate and needy right off the bat. Those traits could come to light later. Much later.

She made her way to the costume room, only glancing at some of the scenes being played out in the medical play area and the water space. Remembering what she'd been able to see on the night of the roulette game, she wondered if she would ever have the guts to ask Tate for some of that play. She'd never thought of using a dunk tank for breath play, but now that she'd seen it, she wanted it.

The costume room was busy with another couple searching for baby doll outfits when Sydney arrived. The little kitty sub who worked the room handed over a bundle of onesie costumes and baby doll nighties before heading over to Sydney.

"I think there's a box here for me." Sydney folded her hands in front of her, trying not to fidget. Did he get her a sexy dress? A nightie? Was he into age play himself and left her a onesie? She couldn't do that, could she? No, not even for Tate could she do that. It was a fine kink, but not for her.

"Yeah. Tate left it for you." She scampered away, giving a thumbs-up to the woman now having her hair braided by her Daddy as she passed them.

They looked so at ease with each other, so loving.

Let's just get through this evening before you start saddling up the white horse to ride off into the sunset.

"Here it is." Kitty held a box in her hand. A box no bigger than would hold a necklace.

"Is there more?" Sydney looked behind her.

Kitty smiled with a mischievous tilt of her lips. "Nope. And he said to remind you — you are to change *into* this, which means you have to change *out* of that." She wiggled her fingers at her purple dress. "But I fucking love that dress!"

"Yeah. Me too," Sydney grumbled. No sense in delaying the inevitable, she pulled off the cardboard lid and found a bow tie. Not even tissue paper, just the damn tie. "Are you sure there isn't another box?"

Kitty leaned over to see inside the box, and her smile widened. "Nope." And with that, she turned on her leather platformed heel and headed back over to the Daddy and his little one to help sort out bows.

Not getting any help from little kitty, she went about undressing. The dress came off easier than it went on. Wasn't that always the case with sexy dresses?

By the time she folded her panties on top of the dress, and slid out of her shoes, she could feel a looming presence behind her.

"Need help?" That baritone could only belong to one man.

"Nope, I got it." She didn't turn around to face him as she played with the bow tie. There was no clasp for it to open and go around her neck, so she ended up tugging it over her head and straightening it around her throat. A little tighter than she would like, but manageable.

Picking up her pile of clothes, she held them in front of her and spun around to greet him.

His eyebrows raised, and the corner of his mouth lifted. "You have it on wrong." He pointed to the black bow nested against her neck.

She rolled her eyes. "How can it be on wrong?" She may lose

some of her smarts when it came to dealing with him, but she knew how to put a necktie around her neck.

His own eyes darkened. "So much to talk about." He shook his head. "First, let's fix this." He reached over to the bowtie and pulled the stretchy band, maneuvering it up over her face and rested it on top her head.

"It's a headband?" She lifted one hand to touch the bow.

He gave a soft chuckle and tweaked her ear. "Yeah. Now about these." He took the bundle of clothes from her arms and walked over to the kitty, handing them off to her and returning to Sydney. "You won't need those."

"I don't think I needed the headband either." She put her hand on her hip.

"Of course, you do." He wrapped his hand around the nape of her neck, pulling her closer to him. "Because I like it. And you like doing it for just that reason." His other hand cradled her face as his lips came down to meet hers.

Harsh, hot lips captured hers, removing all irritation about her nudity at first contact. When he pulled away, he gave her a quick peck on her cheek and looked at her with wide, dilated eyes.

"Was I wrong?" How did he do that, make his voice dip even lower?

"No." She answered on a breath. He'd pegged it pretty good.

"Of course not." He released her face and laced his fingers in hers. "Let's get to the good stuff."

Sydney tried not to let her full nudity bother her as he walked her through the play spaces, seemingly taking a detour before bringing her to the bar area. She could sense glances her way, but she reminded herself there were plenty of naked bodies in the room, and some of them were contorted into much more provocative poses than just walking through the room.

The headband bit at her hair some, but she didn't move it. He put it there because he wanted it there, and she wouldn't take it off. Not yet at least.

He guided her over to a table and took a seat, pulling her to sit on his lap. Cuddling didn't do much for her, but she had promised herself she'd give him a chance.

"Since you're here, and you followed my instructions, I assume that means you've agreed to take this outside the club as well as inside?"

"Yep." She nodded, wiggling on his knee until she found a comfortable spot.

"What was that?" He turned his head and pointed to his ear.

She rolled her eyes. "Yes, sir."

"Hmm." He opened his legs wide, letting her slip between them and pushed her to the ground in front of him. "On your knees."

She grunted from the force of her bare knees hitting the flooring, but managed to get situated without cursing at him.

"I think we should start off on the right foot, Sydney. So, I'm going to be very blunt. I know you've seen me play, you've seen what I expect from my subs, and what happens when they don't meet those expectations. But, let's be clear."

He cupped her chin again, pulling her face upward, and waited until her eyes connected to his.

"You will always answer properly when I ask a question, with respect. No eye rolling, no bratty come back. I have a few suspicions about your bratty mouth, but we'll see if I'm right by the end of the night."

"If you dislike me so much, why did you ask me here?" She narrowed her eyes, digging her nails into her palms at her sides. As a start, it was faltering. Her nerves would be her undoing if she didn't get a grip on herself.

"I don't dislike you at all." He clarified, maintaining his stoic demeanor. "Here's the deal." He let her go and leaned back in his chair, picking some items from the table she hadn't noticed at first. "If you roll your eyes, I'll take away your sight." He held up a thick black blindfold. "If you can't control your mouth, I'll do that for you." He showed her the red rubber ball-gag before placing it next to the blindfold on the table. "And if your hands are in the way, I'll take care of that, too." He showed her the leather cuffs and dropped them on the table. The resounding thunk of the D-rings rattled around her head.

She swallowed and continued to stare at him, for the first time in a long time, unsure of what to say.

"You'll stay down there on your knees until you've been a good girl, then I'll let you sit in my lap."

"I've been a good girl. I put on this thing for you." She snapped the headband on her head.

He sighed. "And you were a bad girl when on my lap. I want to play with you tonight. I want to give you a peek at something inside of yourself I think you've been hiding from me—and probably yourself too—but I can't if you don't behave. You use your snark and your brattiness as defenses. If I get too close to something you don't want to explore, you bite back. I'm going to help with that."

She rolled her eyes and huffed. "I don't need to be fixed."

He shook his head, though didn't look as disappointed as he may have wanted her to think as he picked up the blindfold. "Didn't even make it three minutes."

She cursed to herself as the material was dragged over her eyes, blacking out the room.

CHAPTER 6

*T*he moment she realized he noticed her error, and wasn't going to let it slide, her eyes widened. He only had a moment to enjoy it as the blindfold went on. Her lips screwed up into an angry pout, which he found fucking adorable. The woman had no idea the power she held, but that was okay. He'd show her.

He inhaled the lavender scent of her shampoo as he finished knotting the fabric behind her head. She'd left her brown hair down, thick curls cascading around her shoulders. He gathered the thick strands and brought them behind her, letting it all roll down her back.

"There." He patted her head and sat back in his chair. Her tongue darted out from between her lips, licking at them before her teeth bit into the plump flesh of her bottom lip. So many things she probably wanted to say. He fingered the ball gag, letting the buckle jangle on the table to tease her. It resulted only in making his pants more uncomfortable than they already were.

"Now what?" she asked.

He leaned forward. "Now, we talk, and if you're really good, we'll play."

"I thought playing is what we came here for." She turned toward the sound of his voice.

"Oh, Sydney." He patted her head again. "We are here for whatever I want us to be here for."

"That doesn't sound fun." Her lips puckered into another pout.

"Oh, sure it does." He leaned closer to her still, letting his breath hit her face. Her lips parted and again she licked at them. "Because this time, you are going to play without having to brat your way into a spanking."

"I don't do that." She scooted away from him.

"You sure as hell do. It's an easy tell, and I'm not sure why no one's picked up on it before. Maybe they just liked giving you a spanking, maybe they just liked watching your ass cheeks bounce beneath their hands. But it's not enough for you, is it, Sydney?" He traced the outline of the blindfold with his fingers, watching her chest raise and fall with her quickened breath. "You want more, but you don't want to ask for it. You want it given."

"You aren't making any sense."

He imagined her eyes rolling behind the blindfold. She knew what he said was true, but she wasn't ready to admit it. That was okay, he had all night. And he would get that admission from her. Going further as a real couple wouldn't be possible if she kept fighting what she really wanted.

"Do you like being spanked?" He placed his hands on her shoulders, not allowing her an inch to get away.

She scoffed and squirmed in his hands. "Yeah."

"And do you like a soft spanking or a hard one? One that leaves your ass hot for hours, leaves you second guessing sitting for at least a day?"

Her muscles tensed beneath his hands. Finally, he was getting somewhere.

Unable to move beneath his grip, she raised her hands and tried to shove his away.

He tsked his tongue. "Now, now. There go the hands." He

grabbed the cuffs from the table and made quick work of squatting behind her to bind her wrists with them. The loud snap of the rings connecting sent a visible shiver through her body. After placing a kiss to the top of her head, right next to the black bow, he retook his seat. "How's that?"

Her nostrils flared with a hard exhale. "Fine."

"The gag is next, Sydney," he warned.

She sucked in her bottom lip, biting down hard before she released it. "It's fine, sir." She clenched her jaw.

"Good. Now answer my question. Do you like a soft spanking or a hard one?"

"Why don't you just get to it, and find out? Or are you afraid you can't give me what I want?"

He let out a heavy sigh. "Stubborn." He snagged the ball gag from the table and pressed the rubber ball to her lips. "Open."

She pulled her head back. "No, wait. Okay, okay. I'll answer."

He held the gag perched right at her mouth. Giving her an inch might give her the idea she can always push that line. But he wasn't an unreasonable asshole either. "Go ahead. And I'd do it properly if I were you."

She nodded. "Okay. Okay." She straightened herself up on her knees. "Uh. What was the question?"

Her grin did it.

He didn't even ask, he just shoved the ball into her mouth, ignoring her protests as he reached around her head and buckled the strap a little lower than the blindfold, careful not to trap any loose hairs.

Her urgent mumbling went unanswered. "I warned you, but I guess you need to be shown the hard way. But that's fine. We're still going to get the lesson done tonight." He grabbed her arms and dragged her to her feet. Tate pulled a red handkerchief from his back pocket and shoved it into her hands. "This is your safeword. Drop it and we stop, got it?"

Her throat constricted, but she nodded.

"Good." With a strong grip on her, he yanked her forward, dragging her through the dungeon toward the piece of equipment he wanted. He'd have access to her back, her ass, her thighs, and she'd learn that to get what she wanted all she had to do was ask.

* * *

SYDNEY STEPPED up when he directed her to, and the flooring changed from carpeting to wood. A platform. She stood on a platform, and the heat coming from overhead suggested direct lighting.

Why did she have to mouth off? She couldn't tell him anything with the damn ball taking up her entire mouth. The corners of her mouth stung from the stretch, and drool was already beginning to pool at the edges. All of her plans to be open and honest with him had apparently been a ruse, even to herself.

"Stand here." She jumped at the nearness of his voice. "The DM is right over there, if you need something just drop the hand-kerchief."

She tried to ask him if he was leaving her, but it came out too muffled. She stomped her foot in frustration.

"I have to get something. Do you want to come with me instead of staying here?"

She moved her head around, trying to find a small sliver of vision through the blindfold. She could stay all alone, naked and on display or she could go with him.

She nodded.

His lips brushed against her cheek. "Okay then." His large body pressed against the front of her chest as he reached behind her. "I'm going to link these in front, I wouldn't suggest testing my generosity though." Another kiss to her chin, and her hands were brought forward, the relief on her shoulders was immediate.

Within a flash, the rings were linked, and she was being hauled up into the air, landing over his shoulder. She grunted at the impact of his shoulder in her abdomen. His hand spread out over her bare ass that was now upturned toward the ceiling. At least he'd been nice enough to cuff her hands in front, making the position a little less unbearable.

He began moving through the dungeon. Other than catching the aroma of leather, and a faint scent of wax, she had no clue as to her surroundings.

She was jostled a bit as he moved, and she heard a zipper open and close, then he was on the move again. She wiggled on his shoulder, but his arm wrapped tighter around her thighs. "You're not going anywhere, Syd, don't worry."

Easy for him to say, he wasn't the one dangling over a shoulder fully nude with his hands cuffed, mouth gagged, and blindfolded! Though she could admit to herself she found herself unconcerned. He wouldn't drop her.

"Okay, down you go." The man sounded downright playful.

Her body slid down his until her feet were once more touching the wood platform. His lips brushed against her forehead. "Here's the deal. I'm going to tether you to the cross, and I'm going to give you a sound flogging."

If he was trying to frighten her, he was headed the wrong direction. A flogging sounded delicious.

Because she had no way of saying anything, she didn't bother trying, hoping he was going to give her exactly what she wanted. She'd seen him play, seen the seriousness of his expression as he laid the flogger across a willing submissive's ass. She'd envied the red marks, the heated stares, the breathless cries of his canvas. Finally, she would get that, she would be getting exactly what every other man couldn't give her.

Her hands were brought over her head, and she could feel rope being pulled through the rings of her cuffs and with little delay she was effectively strung up. Drool started to slip from her lips, so she wiped her mouth across her arm.

"No, don't wipe it off. I like it." He hadn't walked away; his voice came from directly in front of her, and his fingers were toying with the ball in her mouth. "Leave your drool, let it drip onto your chin, down your chest. Let it remind you that if you hadn't been so damn mouthy you wouldn't have gotten yourself so messy."

Ah, hell. Her face heated and for the first time, she appreciated the blindfold.

"Just a little warm up," he announced with a tweak to her nose. She sensed his abandonment. No, not abandonment, because he didn't leave the platform. She could still feel him. Her body knew he was near, not far.

A thudding spank landed to her bare bottom. Although startling, no real pain registered. Another one landed on the neighboring cheek. Again, she grunted from the impact, but nothing worthy of any more than a whimper. She could only hope the entire night would not continue in such away.

A dozen swats in all, and nothing to write home about. She rolled her eyes behind her blindfold and settled in for yet another evening of fizzled apprehension. Warmth covered her ass and a soft hum took over her body, but it wasn't enough. It never was.

Sharp nails dug into the underside of her ass, bringing her up to her toes, and a genuine squeal escaped from behind the rubber ball. A calm settled over her as he dug deeper into her flesh.

"Warm-up's done." A fingertip swiped away some saliva from her chin and rubbed it into her shoulder.

Before she could register how she felt, the nails were gone, and so was he. Sydney turned her head to the side, gauging his whereabouts by sound. A scream from somewhere behind her, the sharp snap of a whip around the same area, and an orgasm being shouted too deep in the dungeon for her to pinpoint, but no sound suggesting where Tate stood.

A fire lit up across her ass, and she jumped to attention. Another stripe landed just below the first, and she groaned. Long gone was the thud of the warm up, that thin line of pain couldn't be inflicted by anything thuddy. A cane? A whip? She couldn't tell, but her mind didn't care. The craving was being fed, and she leaned into it.

Suddenly it stopped. Her mind reeled back to the present, to the sounds surrounding her, the cool air of the room moving across her naked body. She stomped her right foot. She was almost there. Almost in flight.

"Cool down, baby. I'm not done with you, but remember there's a lesson for tonight. You have to tell me what you want. Do you want me to go harder or softer?" His silken voice brought the embers of her annoyance to a gentle simmer. His fingers were again on her, stroking what she assumed might be welts across her ass. "If you want me to go harder raise your right leg, if you want me to go back to soft and thuddy, lift your left leg."

Again, he swiped across her chin, cleaning off her saliva. The bite in her ass had wiped away any concern she'd had about her drooling. Her jaw didn't even ache anymore, thanks to the buzz of her ass. But he wanted an answer. He wanted her to choose the setting, the strength.

"Left for thuddy and soft. Right for harder. You still have your hanky if you need me to stop." He ran his hand over her head, petting her hair down her back. "I need your answer, Sydney."

She clenched her eyes closed. It should be easy, just lifting a damn leg. But lifting her leg meant more; it was an admission.

"Three seconds then I decide." It wasn't much of a threat; he barely sounded irritated.

She turned her face away from him. He would have to do this, she couldn't. Not yet.

"Okay, then." He patted her shoulder and moved away again.

Another soft slap to her ass, a few thuds of what could have been a rabbit fur duster washed across both ass cheeks. As sensation play, it built anticipation, but what she wanted, what her body and mind craved, was further away than rabbit fur.

"You're frustrated." He said, swiping the implement across her thighs, only giving her a tiny bite of pressure. "Just lift your leg, Sydney. I'm not even making you say the fucking words, just lift your goddamn leg." His irritation showed. "I know what you want, you know it, too. No need to act like a brat, no need to act out, just lift your fucking leg."

She shook her head. She couldn't. No. She wouldn't. If he claimed to know what she wanted, why wasn't he giving it to her?

The strokes became even softer. Half a dozen, then a resounding slap jerked her body forward and made her grunt. She nodded, meaning to encourage, but the soft fur returned.

After three rounds of this, she stomped her foot. Enough already!

"Right leg or left leg, Sydney." His nails dug into her again. She sucked in her breath. "I can continue with this rabbit flogger, but to be honest I think we are both pretty bored with it."

She tensed. Her breath hitched.

"I'll sweeten the deal. You give your answer, you admit to what you want, and I'll take out the ball gag. You can scream your heart out as my flogger—the leather one I love—bites into your flesh."

Still she wasn't sure she could do it.

"Do you think you're the only woman in this room that loves the pain? That gets off on the heat of the cane, the fire of the whip, or the burn of the paddle?"

His words hit harder than the fucking rabbit flogger.

"Admit it, admit to loving the sting, the fire, and I'll give it to you. But you keep hiding, pretending you don't love the spank-ings, love the discipline, and you'll get nothing but being cared for with gentle gloves."

She swallowed, sucking as much of her drool back into her mouth as she could. The blindfold was wet, from her tears or her sweat?

His body pressed against her back, his chin rested on her shoulder. "It's okay, baby. I'm not going to let you fall. Give your-self what you want." Give herself? Wasn't that his job?

She groaned when his tongue trailed across her neck.

"Left leg or right leg, Sydney." His hand reached up into her hair, fisting into her scalp and pulling her head back. "You're safe with me, Syd."

Tears slipped from her eyes, soaking right into the black blindfold. Her legs shook, but she swallowed hard and tried to give a nod.

He shifted, giving her room to move her legs. Gathering all of her strength, she slowly lifted her right leg from the platform.

"Higher." He gripped her hair tighter, giving her the bite she wanted.

She lifted her leg until it was completely off the ground and perpendicular to her hips.

"Such a good girl." The growl in his voice sent a shiver down her spine, as though she'd just unlocked a beast that had been waiting patiently. The buckles on the gag were opened, and he worked the ball out of her mouth. Instantly she closed her lips and licked away the extra drool while working her jaw to ease the ache. "You know the colors, right?"

"Yes, sir." She nodded.

He squeezed her ass. "Beautiful," he whispered then released her.

She sucked in her lower lip, readying herself for whatever came next.

Her screams rang through the dungeon as a white flame crossed over her ass. Little delay before the next. Almost thuddy, but still full of heat. The flogger landed over her ass again.

"Stick it out for me a little, Syd." He called out to her between laying the flogger over her thighs then her ass. She wiggled her feet until she was able to arch her back enough to give him what he wanted, what she wanted.

Again and again, the falls of the flogger struck her upturned ass, and each time her mind reeled into a blizzard of pleasure and release.

She reached her hands to find the rope tethering her to the cross and held on while he worked her ass and thighs with another round.

"Ah fuck!" She screamed out when the flogger hit the same spot for the third time, taking the pain to a new level.

He stopped, and was at her side running his fingertips down her back. "You are doing so fucking good, baby," he whispered, placing kisses to her bare shoulder. "I want to mark your back. Can you take that for me?"

She nodded without hesitation. A new experience, a new burn. She welcomed everything he wanted to give her now. Because he wouldn't let her fall, she knew it.

"Your hair's in the way." He moved behind her and parted her long hair, pushing it over her shoulders until it all fell forward. She moved back from the cross enough for it to fall over her breasts. "So pretty this way. Tied up, ass bright red, and submissive. So beautifully submissive." He pinched her ass until she squeaked then patted her. "Ready, set, go." She imagined the shit-eating grin he was wearing just by the joviality in his voice.

The hard thud of all the falls landing across her shoulders pushed her into the cross, but she righted herself again and prepared for the next strike. It came harder. The next brushed the tips across her back, the sting bit into her, making her cry out. But again, she righted herself and waited for the next.

The thick fog came barreling into her mind as the flogging continued. She heard herself grunting, crying out, and she heard the encouraging words from Tate, but none of it stopped her from tipping into the oblivion she'd always teetered on.

"Sydney, baby, so good, you did so good." His soft voice eased her back from the fly zone. Her back hurt, sore, her ass on fire, she rested her head on her arm.

The rope came loose, and her arms fell to her sides. He caught her though, scooped her up in his arms. She heard him mutter something to someone off to the side, but she didn't pay attention. Her head fell into his chest, and she sighed happily.

They were sitting together in the same chair. The blindfold loosened as he untied it and slipped it off her eyes. She blinked a few times, letting her eyes get used to the dim lighting of the dungeon, then she turned them on Tate.

He watched her, a crease in his brow.

"I'm good," she assured him and rested her head on his chest. "So, good." Better than good, best she'd been in forever.

His chest vibrated when he laughed. "I know what will make you feel even better." He shifted her on his lap, pushing her left leg off his lap until her legs were spread.

She tightened her hold on his neck when his fingers brushed over her clit. "So fucking swollen, and ready to be touched." He kissed her cheek, nibbled on her lip as his finger danced over and around her clit. "Do you want to come, Sydney. Do you want me to make your world shatter?"

"Fuck yes." She nodded, not looking at him, but arching her hips just enough toward his hand.

"Can you ask? Be a good girl and ask me for what you want?"

His fingers flicked her clit, and she threw her head back, another touch like that and she wouldn't be able to ask anything.

"Yes. Yes, please." She nodded, holding onto him with all her might and enjoying his teasing between her legs.

"Ask then."

"Please, Tate, please make me come." The lingering fog gave her a new bravado.

"Quick learner, I love it." He kissed her again and thrust two fingers into her pussy. She cried out and arched up toward his hand, her left foot giving her the leverage she needed.

"Harder," she pleaded.

He plunged harder into her, his palm slamming into her clit as he did so.

"Oh, fuck." She threw her head back, exposing her neck to his kisses.

"Come for me, Sydney. Come loud, don't hide it." He quickened his pace, hardened his thrusts.

It took no time at all before she gave him exactly what he demanded. She screamed, making her throat ache with the pressure of her voice. The waves of pleasure didn't just crash into her, they bombarded her, leaving her breathless and weightless. As the pleasure began to slowly ebb, his fingers slowed their ministrations. Finally, he pulled out of her, and brought his fingers to her lips.

"Clean me." He ordered and pressed his digits into her mouth. She sucked his fingers, bringing her eyes to his. Pleasure. Acceptance. Her heart twisted and tears again came to her eyes.

Once he was clean, he cupped her chin. "Good or bad?" he asked, wiping a lone tear from her cheek.

"Good. I think." She snuggled into his chest. "I just need a minute, then I can get off you."

"Take all the time you need," he assured her, wrapping her arms around him. "I'm taking you back to my place tonight."

"I have a ride," she told him. It had been a good night. She didn't want to over step, and she didn't want to take too much.

"Don't you want to come home with me?" His arms stiffened around her body.

Of course. She could feel his erection pushing into her hip. "It's not that," she closed her eyes, so sleepy. "We can go into the privates if you want to fuck."

He growled and hugged her tighter. "I don't give a fuck about my cock right now, Sydney. I asked you if you wanted to come home with me tonight."

The irritation crept back into his voice.

"Yes." She breathed out her answer, hoping she wasn't going the wrong direction with him. "And for the record, I give a fuck about your cock."

He laughed, but readjusted her on his lap. "Rest for a few more minutes, then I have to clean the rig so we can go."

"You knew."

"Knew what?"

"You knew how hard I wanted it. How?"

"I'm a detective, Sydney. I can read people pretty well. Now enough talking. Just let yourself relax." He rested his chin on her head and when she started to talk again, he covered her mouth with his palm. "No more."

When she nodded, he released her and she sank into him.

CHAPTER 7

"*I*s your cock broken or something?"

Tate barely managed to swallow his coffee without spewing it all over the kitchen table. He put his cup down and looked across the breakfast plates at Sydney. Her large, brown eyes fixated on him, her long hair mussed a bit from sleep giving her a completely fuckable look and she was accusing his cock of not working?

"It works just fine. Why the hell would you ask that?"

She shrugged, the neckline of his t-shirt shifted, exposing just a bit more of her collarbone. He hadn't given her the option of going back to her place to grab some clothes after they left Black Light. His t-shirt worked just fine as a nightgown.

"Well, twice now you've given me an orgasm, and haven't had one yourself. Last night I offered—"

"To let me take you into the privates to fuck you. Yes, I remember." Not a single moment of the previous night left his memory. He committed every second of her surrender to his mind. He'd seen other women hit subspace, but none of them compared to Sydney. Watching her allow herself to be open to her own desires filled him with pride. It took a great deal of bravery to give over to him.

"You didn't though." She took a bite of toast and ignored the crumbs falling onto her chest.

"No. I didn't." As much as his body wanted to possess hers, he forced his brain to work harder. It hadn't been the right time.

She put her half-eaten toast on her plate and folded her hands under the table. "Why?"

"Eat your breakfast, Sydney." He pointed to her plate and stood up with his own.

"You don't want to fuck me? Is that it?"

If she hadn't asked the question with such a soft voice, with so much vulnerability seeping through it, he might have laughed. Not want to fuck her? Not want to devour every inch of her? She had to be kidding.

"I'm good enough to whip, but not fuck?" The prickle started to invade her tone.

His jaw tightened, and he took a deep breath, reminding himself of his promise to go slow with her. "That's not it, and I don't want to hear that kind of crap come out of your mouth again." He sat back at the table and watched her stare at him. "You don't have sex in the dungeon," he pointed out.

"I didn't say it had to be in the dungeon, when we got home."

"When we got home the last thing you needed was me pawing at you. You needed sleep."

"Don't you think I should have a say in what I needed?"

He eyed her silently for a moment. "You think we should have had sex because you operate under the delusion that I didn't get exactly what I wanted out of our scene. You think that because I didn't come, I didn't love it."

She pushed her plate out of the way and leaned her elbows on the small round table. "That's been the general consensus in my past relationships, yeah."

He leaned forward. "You've been dating assholes."

Her eyes went wide. After a heartbeat, her lips cracked into a wide grin. "I won't argue that point. But it still doesn't explain."

"We'll go as fast or as slow as I think we need to. You can't rush it by being pushy, and you won't get what you want if you start bratting. So, I think you need to let this rest."

"Isn't it just sex?" The vulnerability laced with those words struck him, but what really resounded was the fact she didn't see what he did.

"Sometimes sex is just sex, and there's nothing wrong with that." He picked up her plate and took it to the sink. When he returned to the table she was standing, his t-shirt puddled on the table and her hand on her naked hip. "I don't want just sex with you." He finished saying, giving himself a mental high five for not letting his tongue unroll onto the beige ceramic kitchen floor.

"Show me." She smiled again.

"You're pushing." He cleared his throat and grabbed the coffee cups from the table, forcing himself to look anywhere but her naked form. "What are your plans for the day? I'd like to take you out to lunch if you aren't busy."

"Seriously?" She nearly shouted her irritation, but she needed to learn—pushing wouldn't get what she wanted—but more importantly she didn't *want* the pushing to work.

"Yeah, I was thinking we could head to Logan Tavern." He busied himself with putting the dish soap in the washer and turning on the machine. When he turned back to her, his shirt was back on her body and her cheeks were crimson.

"One of your investments?" There was some bite to her words, but the gentle pink on the tip of her nose softened the snark.

"No, I just like their burgers. I thought we could hang out this afternoon. Tomorrow I'll be busy with the case."

"Actually, I have lunch plans with a friend, and I need to look over the file again. I think I want to talk with Mr. Stanley, and I need to find out who his new defense attorney is. He just had a public defender at the arraignment which is probably the only reason the judge actually let the charges through."

Her eyes wouldn't meet his. Topic changes weren't hard to see through, nor the weight her vulnerability had on her. Taking the few steps needed to close the gap between them, he cupped her face and pulled her head back. "Look at me, Sydney."

It took a moment, but when she did, he wanted to kick something. The woman's bratting, her pushing, her tough exterior, was all to cover up worry inside of her. Pinpointing the exact concern would take time. And he had the time. Hell, he'd make the time.

"You trusted me last night to give you exactly what you wanted, what you needed. I'm asking you for the same now. Trust that not rushing into fucking like rabbits is the right thing for us. Let me lead, can you give me that?"

Her eyes searched his face. She didn't pull away; that was a good sign.

"I don't understand it, though."

"I know you don't. But you will. There's going to be more to us than sex. And I don't think you've had that before."

Understanding lit up her eyes. "Our lifestyle is pretty heavy on the sex, you know."

He released her chin, and stroked her cheek with back of his hand. "I know. And I can't tell you how much I want to get there with you, but first there's some exploring to do. I'll give you all the orgasms you earn, but we won't fuck until we are both ready."

"You're not a virgin, are you?"

He let himself laugh and pulled her close to his chest for a tight hug. "Fuck no. But, I told you, I want more than just sex with you."

She pushed back against him and tilted her head up to look up at him. "Does that mean I can't give you an orgasm, too?"

His cock reacted to the sultry tone she used, and her body pressed up against him didn't do much to calm him down. "What did you have in mind?"

"Well, I can't have lunch with you today, but maybe you could feed me breakfast, something a little more than scrambled eggs and toast?" She licked her lips and let them part.

"Are you asking to suck my cock?"

"Yes, sir."

"Ask appropriately, then." He dropped his hands to his sides and took a step back.

She slid to her knees, removing the shirt again, and tossing it onto the table.

"Hands palm side down on your thighs, spread your knees and get your ass off your heels." Full dom mode kicked in, and from the glimmer in her eyes, her submissive side was in attendance.

She looked up through dark lashes. "May I please suck your cock?"

"No. Try again." He moved a step closer, the bulge in his jeans directly in front of her face.

"May I please suck your cock, sir?"

"Better." He swiped his hand over her hair, smoothing down some of the stray flyways. The more discombobulated she looked, the harder his cock grew. The leftover mascara from the night before, smeared beneath her eyes, nearly undid him. It would be even more smudged by the time he finished with her. "Now, unbuckle my belt, unbutton and unzip my jeans, and pull my cock out, but don't put your mouth on it yet."

Her throat worked when she swallowed, but her eyes widened with hunger.

With agile fingers, she worked his belt undone, nearly giddy from the jingling of the buckle, and went straight for the button and zipper of his jeans. He'd slept in his boxers while cradling her in his bed all night, but she didn't let those get in her way. Her hand disappeared into the opening, and wrapped around his shaft. He groaned when her warm hand held his cock, and she pulled it free of the restraining clothing.

He looked down at her eyes fixated on his bobbing dick, right at her mouth, but she didn't touch. Though she looked ready to pounce if he made her wait too long.

"You asked me to feed you, is that, right?"

"Yes, sir." She inched a little closer.

"Put your hands behind your back, clasp them there. I want your mouth open. I'll feed you. You just take it. Got it?"

Her brows furrowed as she considered what he said. She'd been in control every other time, he suspected. There's a difference between giving a blowjob and having your face fucked, and she was about to learn the difference now.

"This mouth is mine for fucking, or feeding, is that, right?" He ran a finger over her lower lip.

She swallowed. "Yes, sir."

"Then you'll keep it open while I fuck it. I told you, I'm not gentle. And I think you like that."

She didn't answer with words. Instead her mouth opened, and her tongue slid out past her lip, making a perfect perch for his cock to slide over. His eyes nearly crossed with her silent admission.

He quickly pulled his belt out of the loops, enjoying the flicker of fear run across her face as he did so. That sound, leather rubbing against denim as it's pulled free, always forced a reaction from a sub: trepidation if she'd been naughty, excitement if she craved the burn of his strap. Given what he learned about her, Sydney had a little of both, but her excitement seemed to chase away any fear she harbored.

Fisting his shaft, he stroked himself. More to relieve some of the tension in his body, but also, to enjoy the pout in her eyes when she didn't get to touch him yet. Oh, the ways he could deny her if her mouth started to run off too often.

"Open wider." He brought the head of his cock to the tip of her tongue and as her jaws widened, he slid inside, making sure to push down on her tongue until he could feel the back of her throat.

He groaned, and looped the belt around her neck, creating handles for himself with the ends of the leather. "Fuck, yes, like that." He began to thrust into her mouth, stopping only when he hit the back of her throat. "Swallow, Sydney." She did, working his cock just that much deeper down her throat. When she started to sputter, he pulled back, letting her take in a quick gulp of air.

It was a short reprieve. He yanked the belt toward him, shoving his dick down her throat. Her nose buried into his body, and her throat clenched and released several times while she tried to keep swallowing. Finally, he loosened his grip, letting her back off his cock, gasping for breath, long strings of her own spit linking her mouth to his staff.

Before she gained all her breath back, he shoved back inside, pulling her with the belt back onto his cock, and he began to thrust into her. "Lips open," he ordered, and she obeyed immediately.

He could almost smell her arousal dripping from her cunt as he used her mouth. "Fuck." He thrust forward and pulled back to give her another moment to breathe, and to try to gain some semblance of control over himself. She gave herself so freely in that moment, he nearly came just from the sight of her on her knees in his kitchen.

"I'll let you choose, in your throat or on your tits?" He let go of the belt and stroked his cock, needing the touch, denying himself her mouth for a moment. She gulped in air with red cheeks, spittle hanging from her lips.

"Throat, sir." She licked at her lips, wiping some of the spit from her chin. Women didn't always understand how fucking hot they were with their own drool running down their chins while they were servicing their men.

He slapped her hand away. "No wiping." He shook his finger at her.

She rolled her eyes. Realizing her error to late, she opened her mouth and tried to suck his dick back in. But he'd seen her.

"Bad girls don't get what they want. Keep your mouth open and hold up your tits for me."

"I didn't mean to."

"Didn't mean to what?" He continued to stroke his cock, just out of her reach.

"I rolled my eyes, sir. But it was just a reflex, I didn't mean it to be disrespectful." He believed her, but unfortunately it didn't matter.

"I know." He nodded. "Doesn't change that you did it. Now be a good girl and cup your tits. Hold them up high for me." He gripped himself harder, the wetness from her mouth still providing enough lubrication for him to find his fulfillment. Not being able to fuck her throat to completion was as much a punishment to him as it was her.

"I'd rather be fucking your throat, coming in your mouth, watching you swallow every fucking drop. But you had to be a little naughty, and now neither of us gets what we wanted."

Her hands came forward from behind her back and pushed up her generous breasts, a blank canvas for him. His hand gripped his shaft harder, stroking himself faster as he kept his gaze on her. She watched his cock being stroked, with such a beautiful pout he almost went back on his word and let her have it in her mouth again. But she wouldn't learn that way.

She licked her lips, and he noticed her fingers started to toy with her nipples as she watched him. The girl had no idea how fuckable he found her.

"Mouth open, that's a good girl." His release hit him, and he growled with each pulse of his orgasm, watching as his come spurted over her chest. Not a drop touched her tongue, and she pouted even more prettily because of it. When the last bit of come dripped from his cock onto her nipple he leaned against the kitchen table to gather up his breath.

She leaned back against her heels and remained in position waiting for him.

He tucked his cock back into his pants and did up the zipper before bending down to get his t-shirt. Squatting down, he watched her face as he wiped her chest clean.

"I'm not going to give you an orgasm. And you're not going to touch yourself until I see you again."

"More punishment because I rolled my eyes?" She took the dirty t-shirt from him.

"No. Because you wanted to service me. And when you service there isn't always reciprocation, and I think you'll like it this way. You'll tell me next time we see each other."

She took a deep breath. "I really do have lunch plans and need to do some work."

"I know. I'm not punishing you." He helped her to her feet. "So, dinner then, tomorrow after work? Around eight?"

She smiled. The kind of smile that gave him a warm center, as though he'd just given her a great gift.

"That sounds perfect. Mind if I grab a shower before I head home?"

"No touching." He patted her mons, feeling the moisture already gathered on her short curls.

"I heard you," she muttered.

"Just make sure you listen. You don't want that kind of punishment."

Her lips pursed together, probably trying to keep her smart-ass remark in.

She turned on her heel and padded out of the kitchen toward the bathroom. He watched the sway of her curvy ass, the light bounce to her cheeks as she made her way around the couch. He'd checked her thoroughly for lasting marks or bruises and only found a few welts that would heal within a day. But he doubted that would always be the case with his girl.

* * *

"I DON'T KNOW how I let you talk me into these things." Riley sat behind a computer screen typing away. "If Dane finds out I let you do this, he's going to have my ass."

"Oh, I'm sure he's already had it, or at least is working his way there." Sydney leaned over Riley's shoulder and pointed to the computer screen. "That's the guy, Michael Stanley. Can you pull up his visits?"

"Let me see." Riley clicked a few links and brought up the list of check-ins.

"Perfect! Now I just need to do the same thing for the victims."

Sydney went over to her purse and pulled out the post-it note she had tucked away in her wallet with the victims' names and dates of birth.

"Why don't you just get a warrant? It's not like this is classified information or something. Or hell, just ask Dane yourself." Riley snatched the yellow square from Sydney and went to work. "Then I wouldn't have to be breaking into his computer."

"If we find something, I'll request the warrant. Or at least have Tate request one." Sydney scooted back onto the credenza filled with accounting books and other non-essential garbage Dane apparently felt he needed in his home office.

His home office could be photographed for any office supply store catalogue. He had a desk, facing the door, with only his computer on top. He may not be in the military any longer, but his organizational skills still reeked of military precision. Not a file or binder was out of place. If it weren't for the soft blue carpeting, the gray walls, the room would be completely lacking in color.

"You know, you're supposed to be working to put the bad guys in jail, not keep them out. Why don't you just let the defense attorney do his job?" The printer next to Sydney roared to life and started spewing out pages.

"I will put the asshole in jail—if he's guilty." Sydney pulled the pages free and started glancing over them. "And it's a she. Silvia Johnson is defending him."

"From law school?" Riley turned away from the computer to ask.

"Yes, do you have the two victim's schedules?"

Riley went back to clicking the mouse. "Coming next." The printer fired up again. "So, how are things going with Tate?"

The sudden turn in topic caught Sydney off guard, and she nearly dropped the pages she'd snatched from the printer.

"Fine." She picked up the last piece that floated to the ground.

"Really? Because you looked like a puddle of flesh when I saw you last night."

"Hey! We agreed we wouldn't watch each other's scenes at the club." There are some things even best friends don't need to see firsthand.

"Well, he walked right past us with you draped over his shoulder like a sack of flour. Then Dane went to see if you were coming home with us, so I followed."

"Even though I told her not to." A deep voice from the doorway made them jump.

"Do you have to be so stealthy?" Sydney accused, grabbing the last of the paper from the printer.

"What are you two doing in here?" he asked with a raised brow at Riley.

"Nothing." There was a reason Riley never considered a life of crime. The woman couldn't tell a fib if her life depended on it, especially to Dane.

"Really?" He rounded the desk, gesturing for his girlfriend to vacate the area and wiggled the mouse to bring the monitor to life.

Sydney sighed and jumped off the credenza. "It was my fault."

Dane straightened up and turned to them, his arms crossing over his chest as he put on his best glare. "Of that, I'm sure."

She couldn't really deny it. The majority of bad ideas did stem from her own mind. Riley was more of the Jiminy Cricket in their relationship.

Sydney gave him the cliff notes version of what she was up to, and wondered if the same angry face he pointed at them would mirror Tate's. If he found out.

While he had driven her home that morning they briefly spoke about the case, but Tate had told her to let him and his partner handle any digging that needed to be done. She should handle all the legal stuff.

"So, what you're doing is breaking into my home office, illegally getting evidence to prove the man you are supposed to be trying to convict is innocent?" Dane closed his eyes and shook his head. "You know what? I don't care. I mean, I do because Riley pretended to have other reasons to be here this afternoon, but whatever you're up to is Tate's problem."

"You don't know him, do you?" And she thought she was in a tattle-free zone.

"Tate? Just casually. I'm not telling on you, if that's what you're worried about." He went back to work on the computer and logged out of his computer system and shut down the computer. "Now, trash those reports. If you want them you need to get a subpoena."

"I don't need one. You could just answer my questions."

"Well, if you want to have that conversation then bring the detectives on the case to the gym tomorrow when I'm there and ask."

"Seriously? You can't just answer me now?"

"Maybe I would have if you had asked, but you didn't. You broke into my office and went looking on your own." The tick in his jaw made it perfectly clear he was going to be as thick headed about the situation as he sounded.

Sydney stuffed the pages behind her back. Childish, probably, but she'd just spent the last hour getting the information, she wasn't leaving without looking at it. "Just let me look, if it has what I need, I'll tell Tate and his partner to stop by tomorrow."

Dane's jaw clenched, and he looked to Riley. "I'm guessing your computer works fine at your apartment?"

Riley gave a half smile. "Well, it didn't have the login portal like yours has, so it didn't work in that way." She tried a new tack when Dane continued to stare at her in silence. "She's my friend, Dane. I had to help."

Again, he shook his head, looking as exasperated as ever. "Let's go. Sydney, you have five minutes to look, then you leave those on the keyboard, and I'll shred them. Do not take a single piece of paper with you."

"I won't." She crossed her chest with her fingers and kissed the tips. "Promise."

"Riley, you and I are going to the kitchen." He linked his fingers in hers and half dragged her through the door. Sydney probably should have stuck up for Riley, tried to get her out of trouble, but the little wink Riley threw her way as she exited the room made it clear she should stay out of the kitchen for a while.

Spreading out the check in and check out records for all three people she began scanning, highlighter in hand, ready to mark all the times the victims were at the gym at the same time as Mr. Stanley.

Half an hour went by and she'd gone through the records three times. Not a single coincidence between the victims and her suspect. The girls, however, seemed to cross paths quite a bit, checking in early mornings during the week and around lunchtime during the weekends. They arrived and left within moments of each other, yet they had nothing in their personal or professional lives that connected them at any other time.

"You done yet?" Dane walked back into the office several minutes later.

"Yeah." She straightened up, her back aching. "You sure I can't take these?"

"Positive. Come by the gym tomorrow night, and I'll gladly answer any questions you or the detectives have." Leave it to Dane to play it strictly by the book.

"Whatever. Fine." She capped the highlighter and stashed it back in the cup on the desk. "Is Riley still here? Or do you have her tied up somewhere?"

Dane's lips curled. "She's making lunch. You know, the reason the two of you were supposed to be getting together."

Sydney waved a hand. "Don't go all big brother on me. I'm going to head home. This makes me think I need to start looking at other angles."

"Not going to leave it to the detectives?"

"Why would I leave it to someone else when I can do it myself?" She asked, taking a quick peek at her phone. No messages.

"Tate might have another opinion about that."

"Leave him out of this." She pointed a finger at him. "You just focus on your girlfriend."

"Oh, don't worry. I have my full focus on her." He smiled. "In all seriousness, though. Are you feeling okay today? Did he look at your back for you?"

Sydney rolled her eyes and slapped the desk with both hands. "The agreement goes for you, too! Don't watch me at the club! It's weird."

Dane laughed. "I didn't. We could hear you over by the locker rooms. When I went to see if you still needed a ride, you were all balled up on his lap, and I could see the marks on your back."

Feeling her face heat, she hurried getting her things together. No need to relive the evening before. She still hadn't reconciled herself to the fact she'd allowed the scene to get so dark, to let him go so heavy with that damn flogger. And she sure as hell didn't want to think about how fucking good the whole thing had felt.

"My back is fine. He checked me out. I'm fine," she said,

slinging her purse over her shoulder. "I have a lot of work to do, though, so I'm running out. Tell Riley I'll call her later."

"Yeah. Sure."

Dane started to say something, perhaps warn her, but she was already out of his office and halfway to the front door.

CHAPTER 8

*J*ohn paced up and down the office with his coffee in one hand and a copy of an email in the other, while Tate looked over a file folder of pictures from the crime scenes.

"There's a lot of damage to these girls' wrists, where's the coroner reports?" After digging through a few folders, he found one related to the first girl's murder.

"Nothing final yet, but the prelims show rope burns. Both girls have them. Damage from being bound for an extended period of time. We're pretty sure he picked them up at least three days before he killed them," John said and took a seat and sipped his coffee.

Tate read through the report and then picked up the next and read through that as well. The pictures of the girls' wrists weren't clear enough for him to get a good idea, but it didn't look like what he would think a girl being bound would look like.

"What's all this discoloration on her shoulder? The other has the same. Have you talked with the ME? I think we need to head down there." Tate pointed out the purple tint on the shoulders of both girls.

"I'm telling you, we got the guy. This DA is just making it difficult. She's got a reputation for that you know. Always double checking the detectives on her cases. She's a real bitch."

Tate clenched his jaw and calmly put the files on the desk before he leaned over. "You may not like how thorough she is, but you call her that again and we are going to have a problem. You get me?"

John's eyes widened. Tate never spoke to his fellow detectives in such a way. He reserved that tone for the scum on the street.

"Yeah, I got you." John sank in his chair a bit more. "What's with you and her anyway?"

"None of your concern. What is your concern, is that she could be right. Plenty of this evidence looks shaky at best. What sort of rope did they find?"

"Uh. Give me a second." John put his coffee down and started pawing through the sprawled out files himself. "Here. Nylon." He handed the paper over to Tate who only glanced at it.

Tate looked at the coroner's report again. "Did they find nylon fibers in their wrist burns or in the wounds around their ankles?" He took the photograph of one of the victims out of the file and grabbed a micro glass from his drawer. "Look." He held up the glass so John could look, too. "What about the burns on their chests?"

John pulled the glass from Tate and got closer to the photograph. "I barely see anything on the chest. Wait. Yeah, there is something."

"Was nylon the only rope you found?" Tate asked.

"Yeah." John put the glass down and scratched his chin. "But that doesn't mean he didn't have other rope stashed somewhere else."

"No, it doesn't," Tate agreed.

"Let's head over to the coroner's office."

"They had to have released the bodies to the families by now." Tate shuffled the pictures and reports back into the folder.

"Two days ago, yeah. But Dr. Witcomb should have more results back and probably has his final report ready." John gulped down the rest of the coffee.

"We need those finalized reports from the crime scene, too. Maybe we should check out his apartment again, look for other rope."

"I don't think that will be needed." Sydney's voice filled the room just before she entered, closing the door to his office once inside.

Tate felt John tense at the sound of her voice and could understand it. The DA's office could be a little overbearing, and John didn't understand Sydney. He didn't get she was just doing her job to the fullest. She wouldn't put away an innocent man.

"I don't think it's Mr. Stanley at all." She stood in the doorway with her purse dangling from her shoulder, and her long hair pulled back into a tight bun.

"Why's that?" John didn't hide his irritation at all. Not that he tried very hard.

"Because he has no connection to the girls at all. Nothing." She splayed her hands out in front of her.

"The gym."

"They've never been at the gym at the same time. At least not him and either of the girls. The girls seem to have been gym buddies."

Tate watched her lips moving, but the fidgeting of her fingers told him the whole story.

"How do you know that?" Tate asked, taking a seat in his chair. Better to appear relaxed and unconcerned while he couldn't get his hands on her.

"I'm getting the records subpoenaed, or well, rather, we need to go over to the gym tonight and the owner will be able to give us the records. Then you'll have a better idea." She switched her gaze from Tate when his lids narrowed, to John. "We need to find the link between the girls. I think if we find that link we can find the link to the real killer."

"I arrested the real killer." John's teeth snapped together, but he managed to talk through his clenched teeth. "He's sitting in a jail cell waiting for you to get off your ass and prosecute him."

"I don't think he's the guy. I put in a recommendation to my superiors to drop the case against him. As it stands, you have no evidence pointing to him. Some rope and tarps isn't a reason to suspect murder. All you have is that anonymous tip."

"You recommended the charges be dropped?" Tate blinked a few times. Every DA he ever worked with had the respect to at least contact him before doing something so bold.

"Yes." Sydney nodded.

"John, can you excuse us a moment?" Tate spoke to his partner, but his eyes never left Sydney.

"Sure thing." More than likely, John recognized Tate's expression for what it was, and realized he was better off not being in range. Sydney apparently, had no clue what was waiting for her because she simply smiled at John as he left the office.

The room filled with silence for so long, Sydney's smile finally began to falter.

"How do you know they have no connection at the gym?" He asked, rounding his desk and standing right in front of her. His height forcing her to look up at him.

"I'll have the reports."

"Yes, we need to go to the gym tonight, but how do you know now? What did you do? Did you go talk to Stanley?" A cold chill went down his spine at the thought of her locked in a small room with that madman.

"No! Of course, I didn't," she said.

"Then how do you know about the schedules?" he asked.

"Does it really matter?" She tried to walk around him, but he stepped to the side and blocked her. There was no escape for her, and the closed blinds covering the windows of his office kept anyone from the floor seeing them. There'd be no getting out of the line of questioning.

"Oh, it matters. And even more because you don't want to tell me. Which means you did what I told you not to do. You went and played detective, didn't you?" He wanted to grab her when she tried to wiggle around him again, but if he touched her, odds were good she'd find herself face down over his desk and that would be at the very least unprofessional.

"I told you while we're working, we're just co-workers, or attorney and detective or whatever." Her hands continued to fidget. "You said you wouldn't get involved in my work, and working this case is my work."

"Fine. Assistant District Attorney Richards. Why are you pulling my case from trial?"

"Because your detectives did a piss poor job of finding enough evidence to convict, and I'm relatively confident he had nothing to do with the murders," she said.

"There're some weaknesses in the case, I'll give you that. But that doesn't mean he's not guilty." He kept his eyes leveled on hers, holding her gaze. "You said you'd give us time."

"He has no connection to the girls, Detective Tate." She snapped his name like dried up twigs. "He may have been a member of the same gym, but not once in the last six months, since he's been a member, have they been there at the same time of day let alone the same exact moments. They have no other ties, and the motive is pretty much nonexistent if you can't even put them in the same location as him."

"And how do you know they weren't at the gym at the same time? You haven't gotten that bit of information yet. We haven't seen those records side by side."

"Well you should have!" She gave a curt nod. "I shouldn't have had to be the one to figure that out!"

"How did you see the records, Sydney?" His voice lowered.

She threw her hands in the air, almost hitting him as he inched closer to her. "Fine. Fine. Yes, I did my own digging. Dane owns the gym we're talking about."

"Dane Stellar? From Black Light?" He took a step back, recalling the man from his memory. "He's the one dating your friend."

She looked slightly surprised at his memory, but there wasn't time for that.

"Yes. Him."

"And he just let you look at the records of his clients?" He didn't know Dane personally, but he had a solid reputation at the club. Ex-military, straight-laced. It was doubtful he'd let even Sydney go searching through his business files without a warrant.

"Well, not exactly." She at least had the decency to look away from him. "Don't get off the subject. He said if I bring you and John tonight he'll answer our questions and will hand over the records we need."

"You and Riley snuck into his computer and looked." He couldn't help the grin pulling at his lips. Not only could she be a brat, she could be a little sneak. "A real Lucy and Ethel sort of moment?"

"Lucy and Ethel? I think your age is peeking through again." She gifted him with a smile, but he saw it for what it was. Deflection. Sydney may be a year or two younger, no more than that. And she knew it.

"What do you think should be done about this?"

"About what?" She took a step backwards, because he blocked her way anywhere around him.

"Well, about your illegal activity for one."

"I didn't take the reports, and it's not illegal to ask a business owner about his patrons. He can answer if he wants to, there's no presumed privacy for something like gym memberships."

"Well, Dane obviously felt differently since he didn't let you just walk out of his place with the reports," he said.

"Tate."

"Oh, no more detective?" He crossed his arms over his chest again, almost having her.

"You really know how to push my buttons." She stomped her foot. He threw his head back and laughed.

"Oh, honey, I know exactly where they are, how to push them, and when. Right now, though we are at work. So, I'll just deal with the work issue. John and I will look into the schedules. We'll recheck the suspect's storage units, home, and car. I would appreciate it if you could hold off on letting him go free until we are able to do that. If it all comes back with nothing more than what we already have, I'll leave it be."

She took another step back until she bumped into the wall, crinkling the blinds behind her head. He didn't let the opportunity pass, and put his hands flat on the wall on either side of her head.

"Fine. I guess I can do that. But I can go with you to talk to Dane."

"No." He shook his head slowly, letting her take in his seriousness. "I'm going to do the detective work, and you are going to do the prosecution work. Besides, if Michael Stanley isn't the guy, and the real guy has a membership at that gym, there's no reason to go putting your face to the case."

"I survived this long without you being my body guard," she quipped, but in such a soft tone, he let it go.

"Yes, you have. And I'm sure you can do just fine now, but you are under my rules, Sydney. And here's another one. No putting yourself at unnecessary risk. And since you have two detectives working this case, you going around asking questions is an unnecessary risk."

Her shoulders slumped, but when she met his gaze he couldn't find an ounce of offense or irritation. He was definitely starting to find all of her buttons.

"I get it," she whispered. "But I am still part of this case. I still have a job to do."

"Yes, you do. But tonight, I'm going to handle the gym."

He would congratulate her on fighting back the eye roll, except they still had another issue to deal with.

"Now, about the personal issue. Your blatant disobedience, and your attempt at covering up the truth. I might just add disrespect with your use of our work titles to attempt to manipulate me, but we'll see how the rest of the afternoon goes."

"We are at work," she whispered, wide eyes checking the door.

"Yes. We are. I'm going to get John and do those things we just talked about and you are going to go do whatever your brilliant mind does while you're working. Then tonight at eight o'clock, instead of meeting up for dinner, you'll meet me at my place for your punishment."

"We never discussed punishment," she rushed to say, as though the idea didn't really enter her mind.

"When you agreed to be my submissive, you agreed to them. Don't you think?"

"I don't want a punishment," she whispered. Such a simple word sounding so dirty and taboo on her lips.

"Yes, you do. You haven't had one from me before so you think it's going to be all happy spankings and what not, but it's not. You'll see." He pushed off the wall and flung the door open. "Eight o'clock."

She straightened herself up, ran a hand over her mouth, and nodded. "Fine then. Eight."

He watched her make her way through the department to the elevators, and mentally took down the names of every fucking officer who took longer than a quick glance in her direction.

* * *

SYDNEY FOUND herself staring at Tate's front door with knots in her stomach. She'd reached for the bell twice already and each time, her hand dropped back.

Punishment. It was just a little spanking, she could handle it. Hell, after the day she'd had she could use it. A little release would do her a world of good.

She reached for the bell a fourth time, but the door swung open before she could even touch it.

"That's enough delaying, I think." Tate's hard eyes pinned her. No smile, no welcome home, just straight to it.

"I- I wasn't delaying." As a defense, it lacked any evidence or truth. She'd done nothing but delay since she'd gotten in her car to come over. Yellow lights suddenly held the same weight as red lights, and complete stops at all stop signs suddenly became extremely important.

"Come inside." He moved back, pulling the door open wider.

"How'd you know I was here?" she asked, stepping just inside the condo, gripping her purse as though it were a life raft on the Titanic.

"Security camera." He helped her out of her coat, and managed to pry her purse from her before tucking it all away in the closet.

Apparently, being upset with her didn't take away his manners. "This way."

No kiss hello, or a hug. Hell a hint of a smile would have calmed the enraged butterflies tearing at her stomach lining.

Sydney followed him through the condo, bypassing the living room and heading down the hallway toward his bedroom. Needing a distraction, she focused on his body as he moved. The muscles of his back and ass all worked together with every step he took, and easily seen through the tight black t-shirt he wore and his jeans. Well, his jeans couldn't help but cling to him, with the muscle mass he carried. If he really wanted to hurt her, it wouldn't take much effort on his part. But that wasn't her concern as she walked down the hallway of the condemned.

Once inside his bedroom, she stuck to the wall, keeping her ass firmly pushed against it. Silly, she knew it, but still, it would have to do for the moment. She'd chosen to stop home before heading to his condo and change out of her work clothes, choosing loose fitting jeans and a comfortable blouse.

Tate walked toward the king-sized bed, flipping on the night table lights, as though the overhead light didn't illuminate her doom well enough. Just like at the club, items were laid out on the bed: a wooden paddle, a vibrator, and that damn ball gag.

He stood in front of the bed and faced her. "Do you understand what's going to happen and why?"

She'd heard that tone before—more detective voice than dom voice.

"Uh, I think you mentioned something about it." She pushed her hip out and smiled.

"Sydney." He snapped his fingers. "Why are you here tonight?"

She swallowed and took a deep breath. His stare wasn't giving her the erotic chills she was used to when he looked at her. "You said you were going to punish me, but I really don't think we need to go through all of this." She waved a hand toward the bed with a nervous giggle. She smacked her mouth shut. She didn't giggle. Why had she giggled?

"When I dropped you off at home yesterday morning, we talked about the case, isn't that right?" He hadn't moved a single muscle, unless you counted the tick in his jaw. That was moving plenty.

"Yes. We did talk about it." No harm in answering a few questions. Easy enough.

"And when you mentioned doing some of your own digging, what did I say? What did I tell you to do?"

A wisecrack formed in her mind, but the sinking sensation in her stomach vetoed the idea of expressing it. "You said to leave the detective work to the men." Okay, so she couldn't quite stop all of the snark from slipping out.

"Being a man or woman has nothing to do with anything. What did I say, exactly, and this is your last chance."

She'd never seen such stern eyes before, at least not so close, and not so damn focused on her. Her hands couldn't find a quiet place to stay, and they were getting sore from all the wringing she did with them.

"You said..." She took a deep breath, she needed her wits about her—she wasn't going to be some chastised naughty girl, she was a grown woman. Dammit! "You said to stay out of the digging. You said you would do the detective work, and I would do the prosecuting work."

"Close enough." He gave a curt nod and dropped his arms to his sides. "When I give you a direction, it's not to just hear myself talk."

"I know that," she said, but closed her mouth quickly when his eyebrows raised. "Sorry," she mumbled.

"I don't have to explain why I give a specific order or make a rule, but I almost always will. What else did I say?"

Sydney didn't realize what super human strength she possessed until she fought back the eyeroll at that moment. "Because this case is dangerous, and you didn't want me to be in any danger. You wouldn't know where I was or how to help me if I got into trouble. But my point is I wasn't in any danger. I didn't do anything unsafe."

"Is that the point? Is the point of submission to take the rules you've been given and decide whether or not you feel the situation calls for your obedience? It's okay to break the rule, to disobey, because you found the loophole?" He still hadn't taken a step toward her. She remained isolated across the room from him.

"So, you'd rather I not think for myself?"

He dragged a hand through his hair. "You broke into Dane's computer and illegally obtained information."

"I didn't break in."

"No, you had your friend do it. So not only did you involve a civilian in this case, possibly putting her in danger, but you had her do your dirty work for you. But that's not even the issue. The issue is you decided disobeying me was justified. You decided it was worth it, even though every time you do, every time you decide that moment isn't worthy of your submission, you put distance between us. If you're only going to submit when you feel it's worth it, or when it's convenient, then I don't see how this works."

The heavy sensation in her chest took a sharp turn and headed straight for direct remorse.

"Take off all your clothes and kneel." He turned his back to her then and went about removing his shirt.

Her fingers shook as she worked the buttons on her blouse. Stripping away her clothing typically put her in a softer mindset, especially when the man involved promised a hard spanking. It was different this time. Her body didn't crave his harshness, but wanted to be enveloped in his arms. Once she was completely bare, she folded her clothes and put them on the dresser next to her and slid down to her knees, thighs parted and palms down.

He squatted in front of her, wearing only his jeans. What was it about a man barefoot in his jeans that made it sexier?

"Keep your eyes on me, don't look away," he ordered. She'd been staring at his feet. "I don't do bedroom-only dominance, and I thought you'd said you wanted full time submission."

"I did." She nodded. "I do," she added. "I didn't mean to make it look like I didn't. I just wanted to move forward with the case. I didn't think, well, that you'd really care."

"Well," he brushed his knuckles down the bridge of her nose, "I do. And you're about to see how much I care. My rules aren't to be broken, and there will always be strict consequences when they are. Disobedience will be dealt with, no matter how small you think the infraction— every bit of defiance hurts us as a whole." He stood up, and she followed him with her eyes. "Stand up, Sydney, and put your hands on top of your head."

She moved with as much dignity as she could muster. Although his eyes still held the darkness she'd seen when she first arrived, resolve replaced any anger he may have been holding. The tension also loosened in his body. Had he been afraid she'd say she only wanted bedroom fun?

He retrieved the vibrator from the bed, the type that could easily double for a back massager if ever accidentally found. Once her hands were on her head, folded neatly, she let herself focus on him, trying to completely ignore the discomfort of her pert nipples, or the ache between her legs.

"Yesterday morning I told you not to touch yourself before I saw you again. Did you disobey that, too?" he asked, holding her gaze steady with his firm one.

"No, sir. I didn't. I haven't touched myself." And it had been hell. Every time she thought about being on her knees in his kitchen, her pussy clenched, desperate for attention. But she'd obeyed him. She'd gone without. "Is that what the vibrator's for?" She gave what she hoped was, a playful smile. Something to take some of the tension out of the room.

"You enjoy spankings, the pain you get from them."

She decided not to answer. That discussion could be tabled, as far as she was concerned. Maybe he was going to punish her with pleasure instead? She could get behind that theory.

"Spread your legs. No. More, there." He grabbed her bicep to steady her, flicked on the vibrator, and put it directly onto her clit.

She cried out at first, the sensation too strong too fast, but quickly sank into it. "Oh, fuck," she whispered, barely able to keep her hands on her head.

"Come when you're ready," he ordered. Without a current of sensuality in his voice, she should have known. But she was already lost in the throes of a building orgasm.

The vibrator moved up, just above the hood of her pussy. He turned it this way and that, and before she knew it, she was humping the damn thing, looking for the right spot. And then she found it. Electric shock could not have stopped her body from exploding. She yelled out her orgasm, finding his eyes as the hard waves hit her. Completely stoic, no joy or pleasure at what he gave her, just observing.

He took the vibrator away, letting it hum next to her body but not touching her. "Was that good?"

She sucked in air at a racers pace. "Not really," she admitted. Her body had reacted, had absorbed the vibrations and behaved accordingly, but she'd taken no true pleasure. He wasn't trying to make her feel good. He was punishing her because she'd disobeyed.

"Then this one probably won't be either." His grip intensified, and the vibrator went right back on her pussy, at a more intense speed.

"Oh, fuck. Please. No." She tried to squirm away. An aptitude for multiple orgasms had not been a gift she received. The sensation too much, too strong, too hard. "Please. I'm sorry."

"You're sorry you're uncomfortable, but that's okay. Consequences take place even if you're sorry for all the right reasons."

Was that true? Even if she admitted to the heavy remorse weighing her down, he'd still dish out the punishment?

He wiggled the vibrator sending more sensations. Twisting did nothing, he merely followed, and she was too close to the wall to get very far anyway.

"Please!" she cried. But he was not to be deterred and merely began to run the vibrator lower, through her folds and back up to her clit. On the second pass, she screamed out as an orgasm she didn't feel coming burst through her. She stumbled in her stance, but he held her tight, still rubbing her pussy with the vibrator until every bit of her orgasm receded.

She gulped in air, sucked it in like water to a fire. He released her and tossed the vibrator onto the bed. When he turned back to her, he pulled her arms down, cradled her face and explored her eyes. "Now, we can begin," he said, and dragged her over to the bed.

In one swift movement, he was sitting and she was face down over his lap. "No!" She tried to scramble away when she heard him pick up the paddle. "Please!"

"Not so much fun when you've already come, right?" The cool wood of the paddle pressed against her bare ass.

"Tate! Please!" She tried to buck, but he only responded by draping one leg over hers. Completely locked in place. Any semblance of pleasure vacated her mind with the first swat of the wooden beast. She slapped at the mattress, but it did no good. The paddle came down again and again. Not overly hard, she could at least admit he wasn't being a complete brute, but not being aroused made it all the worse.

"I'm so sorry!" she yelled between swats. "I'm sorry I disobeyed!" She cried when the paddling continued. A fire would not burn as hot as her ass did with each new strike of the paddle. And he wasn't saying a word! Not a single word as he continued to pummel her ass with that thing!

After at least another dozen swats she felt the tears starting to spill down her cheeks. He wasn't going to stop until he was ready, and all she could do was submit to it. That was her job, submit to him. And she hadn't done that. It was a simple thing he asked of her, not to go digging around on her own. And she didn't follow, didn't submit to his authority. She'd wedged a space between them because she'd decided not to submit to him when it was inconvenient.

"I'm sorry. So sorry." She sobbed, gripping the comforter, unable to lose herself in the pain. He delivered the hardest spanking she'd ever had, and she couldn't find a moment of pleasure in it. "I'm sorry I hurt us," she blurted out, and the paddle stilled against her ass.

"Again." His soft voice encompassed her.

"I'm sorry I hurt us, that I chose the opposite of what I want, what we both want." She rested her head on the bed, gasping for air and letting the tears fall freely.

"If you don't want to submit outside of the bedroom—"

"No! I do, I, just, I'm sorry, Tate. Really."

"No more digging around on your own. If you have a hunch, we'll look into it together." The paddle bounced as it landed a few inches from her head on the bed. His hands roamed over her ass, but there was no extinguisher for the flames he'd created.

"I hate wood," she said after a few moments of silence passed.

"I know. I promise to only use it for punishments. Although, maybe one day you'll ask me to try it other times." He patted her bottom. "Come on up." He helped her to her feet and stood with her, wrapping his arms around her and hugging her tight.

She sniffled and buried herself into his bare chest. "I don't like spankings after I orgasm," she muttered into his pecks.

He hugged her tighter and kissed the top of her head. "I know that, too. You love the pain, so giving you a spanking wouldn't do much other than get you all hot and bothered."

"I was already sorry before you spanked me."

"You disappointed your dominant." He patted her ass again. "And now you have a physical memory of what happens when you do that."

No one ever took the time to get her head straight before delivering a spanking, and they sure as hell never made sure she actually disliked the punishment. Then again, no one else had ever tried to understand her the way Tate did.

"I'd like you to spend the night, is that possible?"

"Yes." She had a late morning meeting, but even an early morning meeting wouldn't keep her from staying with him for the night.

"Go ahead and get in bed. Early bedtime."

"But you already spanked me," she protested.

"Yep, and now you'll be forced to lay in bed and watch old re-runs of Star Trek." His sexy grin was back, and his eyes weren't holding any fierceness in them. Every fiber of her body relaxed into his embrace.

She forced a heavy sigh. "If I must. I willingly accept my punishment." How could he know she owned every season of every generation, and each movie?

CHAPTER 9

*S*he snored.

Tate hadn't noticed it the first time she'd slept over, but after the most intense punishment he'd ever given, he noticed everything about her. And she snored. Not a loud, wood-cutting sound, but a petite snort here and there. And it was followed up by her blowing out a burst of air through her lips.

He woke up an hour before the alarm to find her making the little sounds, and he couldn't go back to sleep. Watching her enthralled him. So unguarded. Not that she was completely closed off with him. She didn't leave much hidden from him that he could tell, but she still held up a guard around herself. But when she slept, her pure innocence shone through.

She may have played with other doms, and may have even been in a few real relationships with them, but she never gave over to them. Not completely, not like she had the night before. It wasn't something she'd said that made him believe that, but rather the vulnerability he saw in her eyes after he'd brought her back up from his lap. He stayed close to her, making sure she understood he wasn't running for the door.

Her ass would be tender this morning. He'd been hard on her, but she'd heal sooner than she probably would like. His girl loved pain, but she hated admitting it. Did she think she was weird? It still boggled him why anyone, submissive or dominant, would feel guilt or shame over how they felt. If getting her ass tanned got her engines revving, why should she feel anything other than the arousal she craved. But her lessons in that area would continue later.

At the moment, he needed her as much as she needed him.

She rolled over onto her back, exhaling softly and tossing her arm over her head on the pillow. The perfect invitation.

Shoving the covers down just enough to expose her breasts, he licked his lips. Her eyes fluttered, but he was determined. His mouth closed over her soft nipple suckling it into his mouth; he flicked his tongue over it until it peaked.

Sydney moaned, arching her back up to meet his mouth and her hand came up to touch his head.

"No, no, naughty girl, no touching yet." He licked the space between her breasts and grabbed her hand, bringing it up to join her other hand on the pillow. Her eyes fluttered open and he remained over her, watching her as she completely woke up, a smile spreading across her lips.

"Tate," she whispered.

"Shh, no talking either," he muttered and shifted over to her other breast, licking and teasing the nub until it stood proudly. Tate moved one hand to cover both of hers, holding her tightly as he looked into her eyes. Utter openness and excitement looked back at him. "I'm going to play with you, and you're going to do everything I say, isn't that right?"

"Well, what are—"

His hand covered her mouth, squeezing her cheeks a little. Her quickened breath escaped through her nose.

"I said no talking. Already you're being a bad girl." He winked down at her and loosened his hand and let her take a big gulping breath before once more covering her mouth, this time blocking her nostrils, too. "There. That's a good girl." He watched her eyes, flittering one way then the other, her legs kicked out, and he released her.

She took in a several deep breaths, keeping her eyes settled on his. He waited to see fear, and when he only saw resolve, he shifted his body so he straddled her, keeping his weight on his knees so as not to crush her.

"I'm going to let go of your hands. If you get into trouble, you tap the headboard. Nod if you understand."

She licked her lips, already dried from her gasps for breath, and nodded. He released her hands, and plucked her nipples again. She squirmed when he firmed up his grip, but she remained silent.

"I have just the thing for these," he said and hopped off the bed, and jogged over to his dresser. Opening the top drawer, he pulled out the items he wanted and went back to her on the bed. His cock, already at full mast, tightened when her eyes took in the toys he carried.

"Remember, no talking. Knock the headboard if your mouth isn't available, or use your colors." He went about laying out the items on the nightstand and picked up the clover clamps. "These are going to look fucking hot on you," he promised.

She gave a little shake of her head, but otherwise gave no response. "Oh, are we back to pretending we don't like to be bitten?" He tried to put some disappointment in his voice, but truth be told, he almost enjoyed waking up her senses and proving her wrong. "We'll see, won't we?"

He slid his hand down her body, relishing in the soft curves of her figure until he reached the small patch of hair he sought. Closing his fingers around the tiny hairs, he pulled. She bolted upright on the bed, yelping at the sudden discomfort. But he merely shoved her back down to the bed.

"I'm playing. Stop interfering," he chastised. Other than a huff of frustration, she remained silent. If he looked, he probably would have seen an eyeroll, too.

Releasing the curls, he moved his hand lower, sliding his fingers through her wet, swollen folds. "Still a bit sensitive from last night?" he asked, spreading her thighs open until he had a good view of her pussy. He took a moment to yank the comforter off the bed, and then gave her another grin. If he hadn't seen so much arousal in her eyes, the frown on her lips might have concerned him.

He cupped her sex, letting two fingers slip into her passage. Hot and wet. His cock twitched in his pajama bottoms. Kneeling at her side, he continued to thrust his fingers inside of her, but watched her face as he did. Her eyes rolled back as she closed them, and her hands gripped each other over her head. Lips parted, she let out puffs of air.

He reached up with his free hand and took a nipple between his fingers, rolling it and pinching just enough to get a reaction from her as he continued to finger fuck her. Her eyes opened and they locked stares. He smiled, and being the sadistic fuck he loved being, he pulled his fingers out and delivered five hard smacks to her pussy while watching her face morph from divine pleasure to shocked bliss.

When her eyes found his again, her pupils had completely taken over her irises. Her arousal completely over shadowed the gorgeous brown he loved so much. How could she try to deny her love of pain? What a waste!

"Oh, there you are, my little pain slut."

She shook her head and started to scoot her legs closed, but he parted them again. "Either tap the board, or use your colors, otherwise you obey. Got me?" He punctuated his question with another swat to her reddened pussy.

"I'm not a pain slut," she announced and promptly slammed her knees together.

He shook his head, almost giddy from her defiance.

Without warning, he shoved her thighs apart and slammed his hand over her mouth and nose, squeezing her nostrils closed. Again, he delivered five rapid spanks to her pussy and then released her mouth. Giving her a second to take in a few breaths, he re-covered her mouth and nose, watching her eyes as she tried to deal with what he was doing. For a third time, he released and re-covered her mouth, though this time he started to pinch her nipples. She squealed beneath his hands, but did not tap the headboard.

She was gulping in air by the time he released her, and he dove his fingers right back into her pussy. "Seems like your body disagrees."

He pulled all touch from her body, and knelt beside her watching her chest rise and fall to catch up with the rest of her body, and her eyes wandered over him. Anticipation. He could all but taste it on her.

Tate picked up the clover clamps and plucked at one of her nipples. "Deep breath," he instructed as he let go of the clamp and watched it bite into her flesh. She sucked in air and yelped, but didn't stop him from grabbing the second nipple. "Look at me, eyes on mine," he ordered, barely able to control himself from jumping between her legs and plowing into her.

Once her eyes were settled on his, he slowly eased his grip on the clamp and let it devour her nipple. His own mouth dropped open with hers, and his lips tugged into a grin when she let out a gasp of air.

"Good girl." He stroked the valley between her breasts. "You did so good." Her eyes watched him, still full of desire, though a tear slid from the side of her eye. He caught it with his finger and rubbed it along her bottom lip. "I'm going to fuck you until you can't stand it."

She kept silent, only giving an approving nod when he moved to open his nightstand and pull out a condom.

Shucking off his pajama pants, he maneuvered back onto the

bed, nearly laughing with his own enjoyment over her intake of breath. The jostling of the bed made her tits move, and when her tits moved, the clamps made their presence known. He made sure to bounce on the bed just enough to get the same sound from her again.

"Beautiful," he said and grabbed her knees, pushing them further apart and looking down at her red, swollen pussy. Leaning over he picked up the chain connecting the clamps together and pulled it down her torso toward him.

She hissed and tried to sit up.

"No, no no." He put the full force of his body on her, pinning her to the bed, and capturing her mouth beneath his.

Whoever said mornings weren't a good time for kissing was a fucking fool. She kept her hands where he'd put them, giving him full control over her body, and he hooked the chain with his finger, and pulled down once more, taking her yelp into his mouth and deepening the kiss.

"Gorgeous, Sydney. Absolutely gorgeous."

He released the chain and pressed his hard cock against her entrance. She bit down hard on her bottom lip, as though she were preparing. And she needed to, because in the next moment he slammed into her.

She pulled her knees up to her chest, taking him much deeper and sighing as he filled her. Her tight passage clamped down on his cock, and he had to compose himself before he pulled back and plowed into her again.

Waiting had been stupid. He could have found this utopia days ago.

He grabbed the chain again and pulled upward, watching her nipples elongate. "Can you admit you like the pain yet?" he asked.

She shook her head.

"You're so fucking hot and wet, how can you keep denying it?" He dragged the chain up to her mouth, ignoring the squeal she gave from the extra pull. "Here, hold these. If you can't be truthful, you can at least be helpful."

He put the chain between her teeth, and she clamped down on it, moaning as it pulled harder on her nipples.

The harder he fucked her, the more her eyes glossed over. She didn't just like the pain, the girl was near to exploding from the pleasure.

"Do you want to come?" he asked, reaching between their bodies and flicking her clit. The swollen nub was still so sensitive, she jumped at his touch, so he did it again. "Answer me, you can use words."

"Yes! Please, Tate! Please, sir!" She kept the chain in her mouth like a good girl when she answered.

"Do you love the bite, the tension of those clamps? Tell me what I want to know, tell me the truth and you'll get your reward." He continued to thrust into her, but forced himself to slow down.

"I can't." She turned her head.

He grabbed her chin and pulled her back to face him. Wrapping his hand around her throat he completely stilled in his movements. She wasn't getting one more stroke of his cock without being honest with herself and him.

"You can. Tell me. I already know, so it's not news. But say it out loud. Tell me you love the pain."

He didn't apply any pressure to her throat while he waited. The conflict in her gaze started to ebb and he slowly pulled back from her, and slid forward into her pussy. The clenching and heat of her passage made his resolve weaken, but he wouldn't give in completely.

"I do. I love it." Her words came out in a soft whisper. "I love the pain."

"Such a good girl for me this morning!" He leaned down and kissed her, a hard, pressing kiss he hoped she would feel for hours after.

"Please, Tate!" She begged him when he broke the kiss. "Fuck me harder. Please."

He grinned wide, letting go of her throat. "Flip over!" He pulled out from her, and gripped her hips, all but flipping her like a pancake onto her belly. With a rough grip, he yanked her ass in the air. Not a single bruise. Her ass was as smooth and creamy as it had been before he paddled her.

"You didn't let go of the chain, did you?"

"No, sir." She shook her head.

"Let go now, let it hang." He tilted his head to watch it drop, and with it drag her nipples downward toward the bed. "Good. Now stay on all fours."

"Yes, sir." She breathed.

In one swift motion, he was back inside her, plowing into her, and gripping her hips hard. His nails dug into her, but it only made her mewl louder.

"Fuck. Fuck." She started to push back at him, meeting him thrust for thrust. Her tits were swaying, and the chain dragging had to be uncomfortable, but she'd already lost herself in the pain.

"Come for me, Sydney, god dammit come!" He reached around her hip and squeezed her clit.

Just the thing, she arched her back, and screamed, screamed until her body went slack and she could scream no more. The pulses of her orgasm triggered his own, and he thrust harder into her until he made his own sounds of release.

He slipped out of her, and helped her to ease onto her back. Her arm covered her eyes, as she took in large gulps of air.

He took a quick moment to rid himself of the condom and was back at her side, stroking her stomach with his hand. "You did fucking awesome." He gently touched the exposed tips of her nipples. "I'm going to take these off now. Look at me."

She nodded and uncovered her eyes. With one quick motion, they were off her and she cried out, clenching her eyes closed.

"Stings like a bitch, huh?" He chuckled and dumped the clamps back in his drawer and jumped back in bed, pulling her against his body. "You okay?"

"I think you killed me." She wiggled her backside into his groin when she made her complaint. "But I wouldn't mind doing that again, and again." She sighed. "And maybe a few more times after that."

"Well, if you ask so sweetly, how can I say no?"

* * *

SYDNEY WALKED into the medical examiner's office carrying a triple venti vanilla latte in one hand and her cell phone in the other. She'd be meeting Tate and John in a few minutes, and she needed at least five big gulps of her coffee before they arrived.

Leaving Tate's condo had been difficult, not just because she was starting to truly enjoy his company, but her ass and body were sore.

The spanking had been horrible. Not one ounce of her wanted to ever go through that again. The man knew exactly how to get through to her, and that alone boggled her mind. They hadn't really known each other very long, but already he knew exactly where all her buttons were. Putting her through two orgasms before the spanking had not been something she'd ever read about on any of the D/s blogs or websites she'd read. And she wasn't about to start suggesting it out loud at the club either. No need to spread that bit of knowledge through the dominant community.

Not having the arousal mix with the spanking made her really focus on the punishment herself. Typically, she would go through the motions of remorse, meanwhile her body would be screaming for sex after each stroke. But with Tate it had been drastically different from the very beginning. Just seeing the look of disappointment on his face had been enough to crush her libido, and his interpretations of her actions just about gutted her on the spot.

He wasn't taking their relationship lightly. He actually meant what he said, and he expected obedience. She'd always fantasized about domestic discipline scenes. The naughty wife being tossed over her husband's knee for a bare bottom spanking got her wetter than most porn movies she'd watched, but she never thought the reality of it would be so different. His authority and his dominance still soaked her panties, but the look of disappointment, knowing she'd let him down—them down—quickly diminished the effect.

She couldn't discount how fucking hot the sex was this morning though. Her nipples reminded her every time she moved. There was no material soft enough to combat the tenderness left behind by those clover clamps.

She wouldn't lie to herself and say she didn't like it. No, Tate had finally dragged that truth out of her, and it wasn't going to be stuffed back down into hiding. The bite of the clamps had thrown her into a new level of pleasure. Of course, Tate knew that it would be just the thing to bring her to the edge. Hell, he seemed to know more about her than she did these days.

"Oh good! You're here already." John walked in with less than an appreciative smile. "Have you seen Dr. Witcomb yet, or did you actually wait for us?"

It had only been a few hours, yet the sight of Tate walking toward them sent a shiver through her body. He wore a buttoned-down shirt under his leather jacket. As he walked, the jacket swayed a bit, exposing his badge tethered to his belt and his weapon nestled in his holster, perfectly positioned so his hand could just reach in and draw it should the need arise. She remembered his hands on her body that morning. The strength in them as he had cut off her air through her mouth, pinching her nipples until stars danced in her vision.

"Hey," she squeaked. Clearing her throat, she greeted him again. "Hi."

He didn't say anything, but he did grin, a lazy curl to his full lips as his eyes roamed over her, slowly taking her in. Being somewhat rushed, she hadn't wound her hair into her usual bun. It hung loose around her shoulders, sporting her natural curls. His eyebrows raised a fraction when his gaze made its way down to her pants. It hadn't felt much like a pencil-skirt sort of day, so she opted for leggings and a sweater. She'd hoped, and could see in his eyes that she was right—the knee-high leather boots were what put that fire in his sexy eyes.

She sipped her coffee, trying to hide her smile.

John looked between the two of them and rolled his eyes. The cat had jumped out of the bag apparently, and he was no more thrilled with the revelation than he was about her working the case by their side.

Well, too bad for him. Being with Tate had nothing to do with her wanting the case handled correctly, but it did give her more confidence it would be processed appropriately.

"Detective Tate!" Dr. Witcomb burst through the front doors of the building, juggling a box and what could only be his lunch. Anything else that might be responsible for the grease stain on the bottom corner of the brown paper bag was not worth investigating.

"Dr. Witcomb, here let me get this for you." John stepped forward and took the box, letting the disheveled medical examiner right his twisted jacket.

"Thanks, John." He took a deep breath and felt his pockets a few times before finally pulling out a set of keys. "Okay, let's get to it." He nodded and led them down several hallways and a flight of stairs before bringing them to his lab.

Sydney's first time in a medical examiner's lab had been shocking. The chemical aroma, and the sterile feeling of the room, put her on edge. Dr. Witcomb's lab was no different, other than when he walked into the lab he called out for music to begin playing.

"Alexa, play The Doors!" he called out.

"Shuffling music by The Doors," an electronic voice responded and a soft playback of a hit song began to sound from overhead.

"Now. What can I do for you?" Dr. Witcomb took the box back from John and brought it to a shelving unit in the back of the room. Several metal slab tables took up the majority of the room, and one wall was taken up floor to ceiling by coolers. She gritted her teeth to keep the shiver from consuming her body.

"Well, we have a few questions about two of the bodies you examined." John pulled out his notebook from his back pocket and started flipping through the pages.

"Cheryl Florence and Jamie Henson," Sydney supplied the names from memory.

"Yes. That's right," John agreed.

The doctor disappeared into his small office and came back out with several files in his hands. "Yes. I finished writing up my final report last night."

"Mostly I want to ask about the positions of the bodies. The girls were found in an alley, but had been moved there. They were naked and had already been dead for twenty-four hours, that's what the initial reports stated. But there are markings on their bodies that I don't understand," Tate said.

"There were some unusual bruising and burns on both bodies that didn't quite add up for me, either." He opened a manila file and spread out all of the pictures of each girl separately. "Look, here's what I mean. This discoloration of her shoulders, the right being more so than the left, would mean she was upside down and on an angle. The rope burns suggest she was hung that way before her death, but this discoloration means she was definitely in that position post mortem. The blood settles to the lowest point of the body after the heart isn't pumping any longer, gravity sort of pulls it downward. So, if the victim was lying flat there would be discoloration of the back, but in these two cases, the discoloration appears on the shoulders." He pointed out the dark coloring on both girls' shoulders.

Sydney tossed her unfinished coffee in the trashcan before trying to stomach any more photographs.

"What are these?" She pushed between John and Tate, forcing herself to ignore the deliciousness of Tate's aftershave, and pointed to the chest on one of the girls. "It looks like rope burns." She bent closer to the table, thankful for the brightness of the lighting. She'd seen those markings before.

"They are rope burns." Tate knew what they were, too.

"They criss-cross over her chest, and around her stomach." Sydney chewed on her lip.

"Like a harness or something." John picked up the photo and took a closer look. "There's more on the shoulders, do you think she was hung upside down? Like a side of beef?"

Dr. Witcomb nodded. "I think she—both—were suspended for a lengthy amount of time. Their wrists and ankles took most of the damage from the ropes, but the discoloration is really what tells me what position they were in at the end. He had them strung up and dangling from a ceiling, probably."

"Look at the bruising on this one." Sydney handed Tate a picture from the table.

The doctor peeked over at it and nodded. "Yes, again, such a strange place for bruising. The knots of the ropes were placed at the pressure points, not usually where—"

Tate interrupted, "Whoever did this didn't know what the hell they were doing." Tate tossed the photograph back on the table. "I think I have a pretty good idea what happened before these poor girls were sliced up like they were." Tate helped gather the photographs. "Do you remember if you found any fibers in the wounds?"

"Yes, uh, one second, it's in my report." The doctor dug out another piece of paper. "Uh, here it is, hemp. Fibers from hemp with a purple cast."

Tate nodded. "Perfect. Thanks, Doc."

John finished putting all the files back in the box. "If we have any other questions, we know where to find you." John grinned. "Thanks for coming in early today for us."

"Not a problem, need to get a few reports typed up." He waved them off and headed back into his office.

"Okay, so spill. What do you two know that you aren't telling me?" John stopped them on the sidewalk outside the medical building.

Tate leaned against the railing, crossing his feet at his ankles. "So, the rope that was used and the patterns of the burns on the girls chests tell me they were bound in some failed attempt at Shibari."

John blinked. "That bondage stuff?"

Sydney clenched her jaw. "Yeah, that bondage stuff."

John looked at her, the heated irritation she was used to seeing faded away. "I didn't mean to offend. I know..." He looked over at Tate then back at her, suddenly unable to put words together. "I didn't mean anything by it."

"Anyway, whoever did it had no idea what they were doing. The knots left bruises, which show me they put them all in the wrong places. I don't think he was trying to hurt them by doing it that way, though. I think it was just inexperience. I think the other things he did, those were to hurt them, the bondage was just to immobilize them."

"We didn't find any hemp at Stanley's apartment or his car. Just the nylon rope." John shook his head. "I think we should wait until the rest of the forensic reports come in, maybe they found something that links him to those girls."

"Even if they do, it's not enough." Sydney stood on the step below them. "This case has been a shit show from the start. You have no real evidence. The only thing you have linking Michael Stanley to these murders is that anonymous tip which led you to find the convenient items in his car. Brand new items that match some of the description of things found at the crime scenes. It's as though you didn't really care at all about this case.

You just wanted to bag him and tag him. Whoever was closest to you gets convicted. " She kept her eyes steady on John. If Tate was glaring at her, she might lose her nerve. And she was right about this.

"I know it looks that way," John put his hands up in the air. "But I'm telling you he has something to do with this."

Tate remained neutral in his stance between Sydney and John, not getting any closer to either one as he spoke. "I have the same feeling. I still think Stanley has something to do with all of this."

"I think he has a lot to do with it, I can feel it, but you're right the evidence isn't pointing to his guilt." John nodded. "Sometimes you just see what you know is there."

"I'm not sure you should have him released yet." Tate looked at Sydney. He'd turned on his detective side, though she could still see the warmth in his eyes. Even when he went all business, he still could melt her with his gaze. "I'd like a little more time to look into a few things. Those ropes aren't typically what someone would buy for a kidnap situation, you know."

"I think it might do us some good to talk with our Mr. Stanley again. Now that he's not the center of our investigation, maybe he'll be more cooperative."

"His defense attorney is Silvia Johnson," Sydney said.

"I'll get her information and set up the meeting," John said. "You two can work that other angle." With a wink, he jogged down the rest of the steps and walked off down the street.

"What the hell did that mean?" Sydney demanded once he was out of earshot.

"I think I know what it meant, but I'm not positive."

"Did you tell him about, well, us?" She jerked a hand between them.

"I don't think I had to." His casual grin was back. "Maybe your assistant said something. He told me he tried to get a hold of you last night, but she said you were with me."

"Denise? Well, she knows where I am most of the time."

Sydney counted on Denise to keep her schedule straight for her. "But I don't think she knows about us, not really."

"If she's as good of an assistant as my father's was, she knows where you are and what you are up to at all times."

"Well." Sydney felt her cheeks heat. How many times had she said if it weren't for Denise she wouldn't know what underwear to put on in the morning. "Wait? Your dad?"

"Yeah." Tate nodded. "You don't know who my dad is?"

"Should I?" She tried to conjure up the name in her memory, but nothing came.

Tate's expression hardened. "Senator Nathanial Tate."

"Oh." Her cheeks really heated up with the memory. "He's the senator with that little scandal."

Tate scoffed. "Little my ass." Disgust dripped from his words. "That man put my mother through the wringer."

"I'm sorry, I didn't realize. I mean the name. You don't go by your first name."

"Would you if you shared it with him?"

If her father had humiliated her mother by parading around as many mistresses as Senator Tate had during his short term in Washington, she'd probably have as much disdain for him. As it was, her father had his own problems.

"Probably not."

Tate stared at her for a moment, then shook his head, as though to shake away bad memories. "Anyway, if she's figured out you've been with me, does she know about Black Light?"

"Not from me, she doesn't. I don't exactly run my membership through the district attorney's office."

"Someone's getting cheeky." He smiled at her.

Okay, a little cheek was good for him. Good, because she doubted she'd ever be able to completely cure herself of the bug.

"So, if John knows what the other angle is, it had to come from you." She pointed a finger up at him from the lower step. He didn't need the extra height to tower over her.

He sighed. "Yeah. Probably. I've known him long enough, he knows things about my personal life."

"Great." Sydney threw her hands in the air.

"Don't worry about it. He's a good guy. I know he comes off as an ass, but he's a good guy."

"I don't want to think about this right now." She started to dig out her keys from her purse. "I think we should take the girls' photos and head to the clubs, see if they were members. Do you want to split up? It would be faster, or would you rather you come with me?" She looked to him for his answer.

A knowing grin crossed his lips. "I think we should stick together on this one." His hands slid into his pockets. A casual stance, but nothing casual about the smile. Was he testing her?

"Okay," she agreed. "Should we start at Overtime or Black Light? I'll have to do a quick internet search to see if there are any others."

"Do you still go to Overtime?"

There was more weight to his tone than she would expect.

"Do you, Sydney?"

He was worried. She'd seen him angry, seen him irritated, but worried was new. And she didn't like it.

"No. I haven't gone since Black Light opened. Like most of the members, the anonymity is a big selling point."

The crease in his brow smoothed out. "I don't want you going to any club without me." The weight was back.

"Are you telling me I can't go to Black Light with my friends if you aren't going to be there? You know, I have gone on nights and not played. I don't need to play. I just like the atmosphere, the people." After a long week, if she couldn't get a playmate, just being in the room with the sounds of the dungeon surrounding her was enough to calm her mind.

"I'd rather you not go without me." He changed his words, but the meaning sounded the same to her. "Especially if we find these girls have some connection to the community. That would mean the killer is targeting submissives."

"Do you trust me?" she asked, playing with the zipper on her purse with her free hand. "I mean, I already agreed to be your submissive, which means, at least to me, I'm not going to play with anyone else without you knowing or your permission."

"No. I mean, yes I do trust you, but no, you will never play with anyone else while you're mine." He took a step closer pressing her against the door. "And I don't see that changing anytime in the near future."

Her throat closed as she swallowed. The possessiveness in his eyes when he spoke sent a hot tingle through her body. The tiny hairs on the back of her neck stood up, and her stomach flipped. He made her feel like a teenager with her first crush.

"Okay, big guy. I get the idea." She straightened up, and patted his chest.

He shook his head and took a step down. "I'm going to call Jaxson to see if he'll meet with us and you can head back to your office and contemplate all of the ways I'm going make you scream for me tonight." With that, he laced his fingers through hers and led her down the steps.

CHAPTER 10

The dungeon didn't have the same sense of power with all of the lights on. With no music playing and no passionate gasps filling the space, it just felt lifeless.

Tate ushered Sydney through the room to the lounge area. They were meeting Jaxson and Chase, the owners of the club.

"I still think we could have split this up," Sydney said. He tightened his grip on her hand and dragged her to a complete stop, spinning her to face him.

"While I fully understand we are in work mode, I want *you* to fully understand that *this*," he slowly waved a finger between them, "is a full-time thing. Which means, if you want to get cocky and bratty because you think you're safe in your high-power attorney uniform, tight bun and all, let me be clear: when I say I have a memory like a steel trap it means that any and every bit of disobedience or disrespect can and will be dealt with once the time clock has been punched."

Her eyes went wide for a moment, just before the pink tint appeared on her high cheekbones. "You don't like my hair in a bun?" she asked, reaching up to pat the coiled hair.

"Personally, I love it wrapped around my fist much more than wrapped around whatever you've got in that thing to make it so damn tight. But, for work, I'll let it pass. Besides, it sort of gives you that hot librarian look." He sighed. How easily she could pull him off track with her innocent smiles. "But that's not my point."

"I know, Tate. Point heard and fully understood." She nodded.

"Really? That's it? No smart-ass comment?" Something wasn't right.

"No. Not right now. But I'm sure I'll come up with one later." She patted his chest, pulled her hand free from his and marched over to where Jaxson and Chase stood at the bar. The exaggerated sway of her ass in that pencil skirt of hers would get her planted over his knee, but he suspected she wanted it that way all along.

"Hi, Sydney, Tate." Jaxson gave a pleasant smile while shaking hands. "I'm just waiting for Alexander. He should be here any minute." He checked his watch.

"Alexander?" Sydney looked at Tate.

"His attorney." Tate motioned for a table for them to sit at.

"Drinks?" Chase asked, but everyone declined.

"I'm glad to see you two working together," Chase said with a smile, as he took a seat beside Jaxson.

"I didn't realize you knew each other," Sydney said, folding her hands on the table.

Jaxson nodded. "Of course, our fathers worked together once or twice."

"Oh, that's right. The senator." She gave Tate a quick glance, as though sensing the topic of his father would be unsettling for him.

The doors opened behind them, cutting off the conversation. "Sorry I'm late. Had to deal with a little something on the way over." Alexander walked in a few steps ahead of Sienna. Tate had watched some of their scene during roulette. Their chemistry could be felt even from the distance he'd sat from the dunk tank.

Tate pushed away the mental image of having Sydney strapped to that chair. Oh, the beautiful squeals she would give him!

"No problem." Tate cleared his throat and stood with the rest of the men to shake hands. Sydney scooted her chair over and gestured for Sienna to take a seat.

"I like your bow," Sydney said, pointing at the tiny pink bow being used to hold back the right side of Sienna's hair.

"Thanks." Sienna's cheeks reddened, and she shot a death glare at Alexander, who merely grinned back at her from across the table.

"It was your choice to behave the way you did. Not mine. If you didn't want the naughty bow, you shouldn't have been a naughty girl," Alexander said, while flashing a cool smile.

Sydney's own cheeks tinted a bit more once she caught the gist of the situation. Not out of embarrassment of calling attention to it either. No, his girl was red in the face because she wanted it. She wanted the discipline and punishment. She only needed to learn the correct ways in which to get it. If she wanted to play with humiliation, he'd be up for it. She wanted to role play the naughty wife? He'd buy a special belt just for the occasion, but she had to understand acting up on purpose wasn't going to get her what she wanted. She needed to let him lead them there.

"Well, now that we are all here and accounted for—plus a few extras—shall we see what the great detective and his DA need from us?" Jaxson called the meeting to order.

"The gist of it is this: We have two victims, whose only connection to each other is where they work out. Which wouldn't be leading us here, except both victims were bound in a hogtie position for a great length of time, and at least at the very end they were tilted head down. Traces of hemp fibers have been found in their wrist and ankle wounds."

"So, you want to see if they are members of Black Light. Is that right?" Alexander cut in, moving to stand behind Sienna and placing his hands on her shoulders.

"Yes," Sydney craned her neck to look up at Alexander. Her neck elongated, reminding Tate of how gentle and smooth her skin felt beneath his fingers earlier.

"I don't see a problem with that," Alexander said to Jaxson. "If the questions start to get into an area where I think it's better to make this conversation official, I'll let you know."

"That works for me." Jaxson nodded and returned his focus to Tate and Sydney. He retrieved the laptop sitting on the bar and returned to the table, booting it up as Sydney pulled out the file with the girl's information in it. "Okay, names?"

"Cheryl Florence," Sydney said.

Jaxson's fingers flew over the keys. "Nope, nothing. Next?"

"Jamie Henson."

More typing, and then another negative response. "Nope, not her either." Jaxson shook his head.

"Well, that's not really surprising," Sydney said. "Neither of them could afford the membership. But maybe they were guests of a member?" She pulled out the individual pictures of the girls taken prior to their murders. Both in their late twenties, with long brown hair, and the same eye color—brown like Sydney's.

Tate picked up one of the photos and compared the woman to Sydney. High cheekbones, clear complexion, hair and eye color a match. "Shit." He shook his head and put the photo back down. "You could be her sister." He jabbed a finger at the photo.

"All three could be sisters," Chase pointed out.

"This guy definitely has a type," Alexander said.

"I don't recognize any of them, but I don't work the entrance. I can have the guest lists pulled up, if you give me a minute." Jaxson went back to typing on the computer while Chase stood up to welcome Emma to the group.

With a warm hug and a kiss given, Chase gave up his seat for her. Jaxson stopped his work, and leaned over to properly greet his girlfriend and submissive.

"What's the big pow wow about?" she asked, leaning over the table and thumbing through the pictures.

Sienna picked up one of the photos as Chase gave the abbreviated version of events. Her brow crinkled and her thumb flicked the edge of the photograph.

"She looks familiar?" Tate asked leaning toward her.

Sienna nodded and looked up at him. "Yeah. But not from here. I think I've seen her at Overtime. This one, too." She tapped the second victim's photo still sitting on the table.

"So, they are active in the community. Not just a onetime thing," Sydney said. She watched Jaxson as he continued to scroll through the computer.

"I don't see the girl's names on any guest rosters."

"Okay, so they played at Overtime. What about Michael Stanley?" Sydney pulled out the photograph she had of him and tossed it on the table.

"Who's Michael Stanley?" Alexander asked.

"We have him in custody." Tate knew what was coming and hoped Sydney would behave when it happened.

"Then I think this might be better answered in an official capacity," Alexander said.

"You don't need to be an official informant to answer questions. No one's being subpoenaed to testify." Sydney's attorney voice rang through. At least she wasn't losing her temper.

"No, but if Michael is a member of this club, then his identity is to be protected like everyone else's and giving out his information without proper channels being used would be a violation of the contract he signed with the club."

"*If* he's a member." Sienna put a finger in the air to point out.

Alexander tugged on her bow. "Yes, *if* he's a member."

Jaxson looked up from the computer. "It's not an issue."

Alexander shook his head. "Why exactly did you call me in here on my day off?"

"Because if anything really nasty happens you can save our asses," Chase said.

"Does he look familiar to you, Sienna?" Sydney held up the photo for her.

After studying it for a long minute, she shook her head. "No, not really."

Sydney shot Tate a satisfied grin and tucked the photograph back in her folder. "I really don't think he's the guy."

"We can talk about it later," Tate said, but he'd already come to the same conclusion.

Sydney nodded and gathered up the rest of the photos.

"That's all you needed?" Chase asked.

"For now," Tate answered. "It's been a while since I did any extensive rope work, I may need a name of someone who could answer a few questions for me if it comes to that."

"This guy you're looking for is a rope guy?" Chase asked.

"That's just it. I don't think so. I think he may have been trying, but did a shitty job of it. The knots were all in the wrong spots, the way the ropes crisscrossed their chests looked like an amateur attempt at a chest harness."

"Well, I'm sure I know who to point you to if you need a name." Jaxson shut the laptop and reached over to stroke Emma's cheek. "Emma, you need to head upstairs now. Time for lunch."

"I already ate." She smiled sweetly.

"I didn't say it was for you." Jaxson patted her cheek then turned to Chase. "Upstairs both of you. I suddenly feel the need to get closer to the one's I love after all this murder talk."

"You heard him." Chase stood up and scooped Emma out of her chair, waving good-bye as he escorted her giggling to the elevators.

"Can I get a copy of that photo?" Jaxson pointed to Sydney. "That Michael guy? I'll ask the bouncers upstairs if they've seen him before, and let you know if I hear of anything."

"I'll email you a copy as soon as I get back to the office."

"Well." Alexander slapped his hands together and rubbed them with more menace than Sienna appeared ready to see.

Tate hid his smile. Watching a submissive as she realizes her dominant is planning evil things would never get boring.

"I think it's time we have ourselves some fun. Jaxson, I assume the room is ours?" Alexander pulled Sienna out of her chair.

"Sure thing. You have three hours, then you'll be overrun with staff and a cleaning crew."

"I think that's just enough time." Alexander nodded, bent over and maneuvered Sienna out of her chair and over his shoulder. "I am taking the day off, and we're going to have some fun." With a wave, he carried her off toward the costume room.

"We need to get going." Tate rose from his chair, helping Sydney from hers and extended his hand toward Jaxson. "Thanks for the help, I appreciate it."

"Anytime. I hope you get this guy. You don't seem confident you have the right one," Jaxson said.

"No, we aren't right now," Sydney responded.

"Well, if there's anything else, just call."

"You bet," Tate motioned for Sydney to get a move on, and with the loud giggle escaping from the costume room, she picked up her speed.

As they stepped out into the coatroom, her phone began to ring. Tate followed behind her as she took the call and made their way outside to the car parked on the street. There were a lot of uh-huhs and yes's but nothing to give away who she was talking to.

Finally, she clicked off the call as she stood outside the car and crammed the phone in her purse. "We have a big problem."

"What's that?" he asked, opening the car door for her.

"That was Denise. Michael Stanley just signed a confession. John's been trying to reach you but your phone's off, I think."

Tate yanked out his phone. "Dead battery. What did he say?"

"He went to talk to him, and Michael had a full confession already waiting for him."

"To both?"

"Both."

* * *

"Of course!" Sydney slammed her dishwasher door and fisted her hands on the counter. Always rushing at the last minute, she'd forgotten, for the second day in a row, to turn the dishwasher on before she left for work in the morning. Which really didn't matter because for the second day, she'd also forgotten to stop at the store on the way home to get soap.

Michael signing his confession didn't just present a problem for her, it blew up her entire afternoon. None of her superiors would listen to anything she had to say when she said she didn't accept the confession. Words like 'easy win' and 'don't look a gift horse in the mouth' were already floating around. What a stupid saying. What horse ever went around giving gifts, and even if it did, did looking in his mouth insult him or something? More bureaucratic bullshit at work. Getting the easy conviction. The very thing she fought against every damn day.

Make sure the guilty are put away and the innocent stay free. No matter what side of the line she stood on— defense, prosecution—it didn't matter. Everyone just wanted to sweep these cases into a win column and go get a beer.

"Guess it's pizza for dinner," she said to herself and snatched her phone from the counter, hitting the speed dial for the Luigi's on the corner. It might have been embarrassing to some that when the pizza guy picked up her call, he simply verified her order, not asking what it was.

She stepped over the basket of folded laundry in the living room and planted herself down on her couch, flicking the TV on for background noise and spreading her files out on the coffee table. There had to be something, some reason Michael would confess to two murders he didn't commit. Motive didn't exist and most of the evidence was bullshit at best. There had to be something she wasn't seeing.

The knock on her door interrupted her long enough to remember she'd ordered pizza.

"Coming!" She hopped off the couch and barely avoided tripping over the laundry basket before she flung the door open, a crumpled up twenty in her hand.

"You don't even check? You just fling the door open?" A slack-jawed Tate took up her doorway.

They hadn't talked about meeting for dinner; she would have remembered. Because she wouldn't have allowed him near her apartment.

"I thought you were the pizza guy." She showed him the twenty.

"I'm here, Syd!" Tommy, the usual delivery guy, turned the corner from the elevators carrying her extra-large sausage and mushroom, and mozzarella sticks.

Tate stepped out of the way long enough for Tommy to hand Sydney the box, but when she went to hand over her twenty, he waved her hand away. "I got this." He dug out his wallet and retrieved a few bills.

"Thanks, Tommy." She gave him a smile before he headed back down the hall. "Thank you, too. But I could have paid for it myself." Sydney turned around with the pizza and took it to the kitchen.

"Didn't think you couldn't, but I wanted to." His lopsided grin wasn't lost on her when he stepped into the apartment and closed the door. Nor was the look of surprise when he glanced around the room.

"I – uh – I didn't think we had plans tonight." She casually walked over to the couch and scooted the laundry basket behind it with her foot. Unfortunately, she couldn't hide the five other piles of laundry haphazardly set around the room. To her credit most were clean, just not folded yet.

"We didn't." His gaze hadn't found his way back to her yet. He absorbed the mess that was her life. "You didn't get robbed recently did you?" He half smiled.

Her face heated, and she let loose a giggle. The second time he'd made her giggle! She cleared her throat and reminded herself her mess was organized and not sloppy. "No. Just doing laundry. I've been busy." She gathered up the pile of whites sitting on the armchair. "Here. Have a seat."

"Where are you going to put those?" He pointed to the bundle of panties and socks in her arms.

"In my room. Be right back." She jogged to her room, tossed the pile in an empty basket and returned to the living room.

Tate stood over the coffee table looking at the file. "I was afraid you'd be doing this." He dropped the paper he was looking over and pointed to the couch. "Sit."

"Tate."

He raised an eyebrow and pointed again. "I said sit."

She obeyed, but gave an exaggerated huff before she did. No need to make it look easy.

With one step, he maneuvered over the coffee table and sat down. She wanted to take exception to his sitting on her furniture, except she'd done much worse to it over the years.

"No work tonight, okay?" He opened his legs, and pulled her knees between his, completely trapping her on her own couch.

"I wasn't going to. I was just going to look over the files again."

He laughed. "That's working. You need a night off from this worry. It will be there in the morning. This whole mess will be there in the morning."

"And if the guy who is responsible for these murders is out there right this minute ready to do it again?"

His hands caught hers while she gestured, and brought them to his lips. As sweet as it was to feel his lips against her fingers, it wouldn't do the trick. It wouldn't settle her mind.

"Even if you pour over these files from now until morning, you won't solve this case. So tonight, you're taking the night off." He leaned back and dropped her hands.

"My mind is just whirling right now, Tate." She sat back against the couch cushions. If he came over for a romantic evening, it wasn't happening. Not with her anyway.

"I know." He tapped her chin with his fingers. "And I'm pretty sure I know how to fix it."

"How's that?"

"Well, for starters you're going to clean up this living room. It's a mess. And then we'll talk about your naughty behavior." He looked around the room again. "Girls who can't keep their rooms clean get really hard spankings."

He wasn't smiling, but the meaning rang clear. Sydney's heart lightened. He knew. He knew, and he wasn't going to make her say it or ask for it.

"I have to clean up this mess? Can't we just go into the bedroom? It's clean in there." She pointed to the hallway near the kitchen.

He shook his head. "Nope, but now you can do your chores naked." In one quick motion, he stood and dragged her to her feet. The space between the table and the couch was too close for them not to be completely butted up against each other. The March weather was getting warmer, and he'd worn only a long-sleeved shirt with his jeans, letting her feel every bit of muscle beneath the cotton fibers. He had her stripped out of her oversized t-shirt before she could bat an eye. "Pants, too." He fingered the elastic of her yoga pants.

She took a deep breath in and leaned into his chest, cuddling up to him with her arms wrapped around his waist. His arms enveloped her, and he pressed a kiss to the top of her head.

He smelled like worn leather. Soft and supple, but strong all the same. Being in his arms calmed some of the background noise in her mind.

"You okay?" he asked after a few silent moments went by. He

wasn't pushing for answers or striving to hear everything in her mind. His dominance wasn't threatened by her taking the lead for a brief moment to get the cuddle she needed just then.

She exhaled. "I'm good. Just needed a second of, well, safety I guess." Now there was a statement she did not want to have to explain. If he understood all the swirling of negativity and frustration running rampant around her mind, he'd probably hightail it out of there before she could finish explaining.

"Well, if you're good, then why are your pants still on?" He looked down at her, raising her chin with two fingers to meet her eyes. "Drop the drawers."

She couldn't help laughing. "Sometimes I think you aren't as strict and dangerous as you play in the dungeon."

His eyes darkened. "Trust me, when the moment calls for it, I'm as strict as they come. I think you remember the other day."

"Yes!" She jerked her chin out of his hands and went about swooping her pants down her legs and kicking her way out of the tight leggings.

"Good. Now pick up your dirty clothes and go put them in your hamper." He twisted around and plopped down on her couch. Sitting in the middle, he draped his arms over the back, giving a royal appearance. "Why are you still standing here?"

"My hamper is, uh..." She pointed to the pile of dark clothes near the television set.

He shook his head. "You don't have an actual hamper?"

"Well, I have a basket." She had lots of baskets.

"Fine. However you do it, get this room cleared of all these clothes. Now."

"Yes, sir," she whispered, feeling the calm starting to take over just enough to get her moving. Being nude didn't faze her. Maybe it should have, or maybe it would have, if it had not been Tate sitting in the living room giving her directions. The little house woman doing her chores for her man. If she touched herself, she knew what she'd feel. And knowing he was going to give her spanking once she finished made her want to touch herself. Just a little.

But she didn't dare. Tate watched every move she made, and he didn't need to know just how much the whole scene turned her on.

It took seven trips to the bedroom—and four baskets—but she finally moved all the dirty clothes to the bedroom, then put away the clean clothes in the closet or her dresser.

"I'm not usually so messy. I've just been busy."

"I think I found your Black Light application. For the roulette game, didn't you say you didn't get it turned in on time?" Tate held up the printed version of the application he'd plucked off her coffee table.

She laughed. "That's where that went."

"How do you function on a daily basis?" He tsked at her.

"Well, I have Denise. If it wasn't for her, I'd probably go to the wrong courthouse."

"Hmm, seems you have been a naughty girl. Leaving the place messy, not doing your work on time?" He waved the application before letting it fall to the table. He sat back down on the couch and crooked a finger at her. "Come over here right now and get across my lap. You're going to get one hell of a spanking, young lady."

She may have squeaked. Someone did, and she assumed it was her because his words hit the *fantasy-come-true* button, but she couldn't admit she produced the high-pitched sound that she heard directly after his instructions.

He had to have heard the same sound, but was polite enough to ignore it. She scurried around the back of the couch to get on his right side and climbed onto the couch, almost diving over his lap.

He did give a chuckle then, and she couldn't blame him. If the pillow she landed on had been home plate, she would have just scored a winning run.

One arm wrapped around her waist, while he tugged her into a better position over his lap. She grabbed the pillow and pushed her face into it, waiting. His hand started to rub circles over her skin, titillating the area with the warmth of his flesh and the magic of his touch.

"Tell me about this laundry problem." He squeezed her right cheek in his hand, pulling it to the side.

Her body clenched at the sudden exposure. "It's not really a problem." She shrugged into the pillow and tried to wiggle enough to free her ass from his grip. He still held her cheeks open. What the hell was he doing? Staring? Planning?

"I think a thick plug right here," he said, and pressed his thumb against the tight ring of her ass, "would help you concentrate." A heartbeat later he released her. "But I didn't bring my toy bag, so you'll have to wait for another time."

His open hand landed on her bare ass. Not hard enough to snap her mind to attention, but it was a start. He began his steady rhythm, making sure none of her backside went untouched, and when he finished with that round, he increased the intensity.

She moaned after one particularly hard swat and he rubbed it away. Frustrated, she sighed into the pillow.

"I think we need to change tactics." He patted her bottom softly. "Get up." She scooted off his lap and knelt beside him on the couch.

"Did I do something wrong?" She grabbed her shoulders and hugged herself.

"No, I did. This fantasy isn't what you need tonight. Tonight, you need hard." He twisted on the couch and pulled her arms to her lap. Cradling her face in his hands he brought his face right up to hers. "I want to show you how much you can take—how much you want to take."

CHAPTER 11

Sydney's eyes had the ability to express every emotion and thought she possessed when she let her guard down. And from what Tate witnessed while she worked and while she played, it was only in the quiet moments with him the window opened.

His remark didn't fall on deaf ears. She knew what he meant, and she had lit up like a Christmas tree only to dim her excitement a moment later. The woman had no idea how much it turned him on that she wanted a hard thrashing, that she could take a hard flogging. Hell, the whipping he'd given her the last time they played at the club had his cock hard for hours after. Just remembering the little exhales and grunts pumped the blood straight to his groin.

Some submissives didn't like to admit they enjoyed being submissive, but with Sydney it was specific. She didn't want to admit to enjoying the amount of pain she did. Maybe it was the label of pain slut. Maybe it was being into the intensity made her a bit more of a freak than the others? He'd get to the bottom of it, but first his girl needed him. She needed the quiet only his belt would bring her.

"You want it, too. Don't you?" He brushed the length of her nose with his knuckles.

"Why do you always ask me that? Can't we just play?"

He grabbed her shoulders and threw her back over his lap, landing five hard blows to her ass, and thoroughly enjoying the vision of her ass wiggling beneath him. When he brought her back up to face him, he put his finger over her mouth to still her.

"I want an answer. I know the truth, you know the truth, and soon you'll be able to say it. For now, I just want you to be okay with what we are going to do. Because Sydney, I'm going to hurt you. I'm going to use my belt, my hand, and anything else I need, to bring you to that place where your mind silences and lets you fly. I am going to do it, and it's going to take a lot, because you have a high tolerance for pain. You enjoy it. So, you have to tell me you're okay with me pushing you. Because, I'm going to push you." He dropped his hand, signaling it was her turn to speak.

She stared at him, air coming and going from her opened mouth, but no sounds.

"Okay," she whispered when he grabbed her again, ready to deliver a much longer spanking to get her mouth to work right. "Okay."

"Good." He nodded and stood from the couch, taking her hand and pointing toward where he assumed her bedroom was.

The room wasn't as messy as he'd imagined it would be. The living room had surprised the hell out of him when he'd walked in earlier. Obviously, Sydney had some flighty tendencies, but instead of being turned off by the mess, he'd found the flaw endearing. Besides, it gave him a reason to spank her lush ass. Spanking the housewife was a fantasy of his, too, but they'd play that game another night. When they both weren't wound so tight and needing a much greater release.

"Do you have toys?" he asked and wasn't the least bit surprised to see her drag a basket from the out of the closet. The woman harbored an unhealthy infatuation with baskets. Most were woven wicker, the others regular plastic laundry baskets, and a few were a bit more elaborate than he thought any basket had the right to be. "Go sit on the bed." He waved her away while he took inventory.

The bed creaked several times as she stood up and sat back down, repeatedly.

Digging to the bottom of the wicker basket, he found the goods. The items she buried because she either assumed no one would want to use them with her, or she was afraid they would and she'd have to admit how much she loved it.

"Have you ever used this?" He pulled out the leather strop from beneath the pile.

Her fingers were in her mouth, and she shook her head.

"You bought it though? It wasn't a gift for you?"

"What? A gift? Who gives a strop for a gift?" she asked, standing back up. He pointed to the bed and she sank back down, and a fingernail slid between her teeth.

"And this?" He stood up, holding the strop in one hand, and showing her the deep purple devil's tongue in his right hand.

"I, uh, yeah, I bought that, too." The soft blush that had started when they walked into the room now burned bright, highlighting her high cheekbones and the gentle slope of her nose.

Dropping the two items next to her on the bed, he cupped her chin and tilted her head back. "You bought two serious toys, on your own, but you still have a hard time admitting you like more than just a little spanking?"

"I already admitted it to you at your place," she pointed out, moving her eyes away from his face.

"Tell me you love the pain, all of it. Tell me how much you crave it, and want it tonight."

Those kissable, fuckable lips of hers moved, but nothing came out. An admission during passion didn't count, he wanted the full truth and he wasn't giving her time to think it over any more.

When she didn't respond, he moved his hand down to her

throat, not squeezing, just holding her in position. "I asked you a question," he said, dropping his voice.

Her throat constricted beneath his grasp. "You might be right."

His hand squeezed, just enough for her to feel the pressure.

"Okay, you're right."

"What am I right about?" he asked, bringing his nose to brush hers.

"I like the pain. I like when you go harder. I love when I feel the fire and burn." Her eyes stared directly into his while she gave him the words. The freedom he'd granted her by forcing the truth from her shimmered in her eyes.

"Stand up, bend over the bed, and spread your legs." He released her throat and gave her room to follow instructions.

She eyed him cautiously, only glancing at the two toys he had on the bed as she moved into position. She gripped the deep purple comforter, and buried her face into it, raising her ass for him without being told. Her feet walked outward until not only her ass, but her pussy was exposed to him as well.

He unbuckled his belt, watching her ass clench at the sound of the metal jangling, and pulled it free from his jeans. Doubling it over, he moved to her side, and placed a hand on her back. "Not an inch out of position, do you understand me, Sydney? Not one inch."

"Yes, sir," she mumbled into the blanket.

He pulled his hand back and brought the leather belt across her ass, hard. She jolted, but her feet remained planted. Again, he brought it down, making a second red stripe on her ass. Again, she stayed where he put her. He made his way down her ass to her thighs and then back up. She grunted into the bed, but remained perfectly in place.

Pulling his hand back even further, he unleashed a particularly hard lash across her thighs. She screeched into the bedding.

"You're doing so good." He rubbed her back. "I think we can move on to this lovely thing." He dropped the belt on the bed, and picked up the devil's tongue. The rolled purple suede came to a point, a foot from the hand carved wooden handle. Not a novelty toy by any means. It would pack a bite.

"Stand up for me, put your hands behind your head and face me."

She moved into position quickly, her fingers lacing behind her head. Her breasts lifted with the movement, and made the delicious target he knew they would be.

"Don't move. Remember."

"Yes, sir." She nodded, but instinctively folded into herself when he raised his hand.

"What was that?" He asked, hiding his own amusement. Her shocked expression over her reaction matched his own feelings on the subject.

"I- I'm sorry." She pulled her elbows back, exposing her chest to him again. "I've never had my breasts whipped."

"There's a first time for everything, but I'm not whipping them." He pulled out two clothes pins from his jeans pocket. "You bought the colored ones." He draped the tongue over her shoulder and went about tweaking her nipples. "I particularly like these purple ones because they match this little whip so well." He pinched the ends of the pin several times, letting them snap right on the edge of her nipple, but never quite grabbing it. "Watch me, look down at your tits and watch."

"Tate," she groaned.

"Sydney." He palmed the clamp and flicked her nipple. "It's sir. Got it?"

"Yes!" She sucked in her breath when his finger flicked her again. "Yes, sir!"

"There we go, now eyes on your tits."

Her breasts heaved with her quickened breath, and he could feel the warmth of her breath on him as he plucked her nipples. Her muscles tensed and her lip completely disappeared into her mouth. Anticipation built, but it wasn't time yet.

"Do you think it's going to hurt? I can just ease the clothespin on and it won't be so bad. Or I can snap it, let it bite into this fat nipple of yours. Which do you want? Tell me, which way?"

She groaned, but didn't respond.

"No answer isn't an answer, and it will only make me want to punish you. You remember what punishments are like, right? Forced orgasms, hard spankings, and that's when I'm being nice."

A soft whimper escaped her lips.

"Do you want me to go easy?"

The turmoil was there, written all over her features, squeezing her muscles and clamping down on her mind. She'd already admitting to loving pain, but asking for it was an entirely different level of self-acceptance.

"Do you want me to go easy, Sydney?" He opened the clothespin and positioned her peaked nipple between the prongs.

"No." Barely a whisper. "No, sir, don't go easy," she said with conviction.

He let the pin slip from his fingers and bite into her nipple.

She let out a scream, throwing her head back and stomped her right foot onto the carpeting, but she eased her elbows back into position. The glassy look of satisfaction ebbed into her gaze.

"How about this one? Should I go easy? Or do you want the bite, do you want that sharp pain shooting through your body, coursing through your core until you scream from it?"

She sighed, frustrated at being made to vocalize her wants, probably, but it didn't matter.

"Say it, Sydney."

She looked up at him, a coy smile on her lips. "Bite me, sir."

He laughed. "Oh. Sydney. You have no idea how happy that just made me." He released the clamp letting it snap shut on her nipple, and before she could get the full impact of the bite, he flicked with the ends of both clothes pins, making them bob, and pull on her nipples.

"Ah!" She tried to twist away from him, but one quick slap to her hip and she repositioned herself.

"Now, turn around so I can use this tongue on your ass." He pulled the toy from her shoulder and was only slightly surprised when she obeyed. "First, jump for me. Three times."

"W-what?" she asked, looking over her shoulder at him.

"I want you to jump three times. You asked me to bite you, so, I'm going to let the clothes pins do it for me. Three jumps. Now."

Her face reddened, but she turned away from him before he could see the full extent of her reaction.

One little hop and he tsked his tongue. "No, no. Jump."

Both feet left the floor, and she cursed under her breath. The second jump was a little smaller, but still acceptable. "Nice and high this one." He mused out loud. He was sure she cursed at him, but had enough intellect to keep her voice hidden from him.

She jumped high into the air and when she landed, her hands unlaced for a brief moment before she made her correction.

"Did you like that?"

"No, sir." She shook her head.

"You want me to give you pain, you want me to lead you through this, but when you act up, when you brat me, you won't get it, and it will suck."

"Yes, sir." She nodded.

Such a pliable girl once he had the right tools.

"Good girl, now stand still. This is going to be fucking awesome." He pulled the tongue back and unleashed, letting the very tip snap across her ass. He didn't quite understand the curse word she threw out, but it didn't matter. The second and third flick of his wrist brought the same reaction.

Tiny red flickers of marks began to show on her already red ass.

After half a dozen, she wasn't hoping around so much. Her bare feet were planted on the soft gray carpeting, her hands remained linked behind her head, and beautiful, musical gasps for breath came from her mouth with each lick of the tongue.

"Hold up your hair," He commanded and she gathered the strands onto the top of her head.

He flicked the tongue across her back, this way and that. Each little puff of air, every little grunt and sigh stroked him, filled him with the sense of power. All of her energy flowed to him with each submission to the pain, and his power seeped into her skin with each stroke of the devil's tongue. He took what she gave, and gave what she needed. There was no beginning of her, and no end to him.

"Fuck!" She cried out and took a step forward, her hand coming free from behind her head. She steadied herself with a hand on the bed.

"Color?" he prompted.

"Yellow."

"Strop?"

"Yes, sir. Please." She put both hands on the mattress, offering her ass to him again.

The clothespins dangled from her nipples so prettily he almost left them in place. "Breathe." He ordered and pulled off the first pin. Her breast elongated as he pulled and bounced back in rhythm with her groan. "And the other." He yanked it off. The snap of the pin coinciding with her yelp.

Already he could see little welts forming between her shoulder blades and all over her ass. He wouldn't give her much more, just enough to push that line. Teetering, for her, would be worse than never seeing it at all, and he'd never leave her just hanging on the edge. Not like that. Not when she opened her heart to him, let him see the insides of her desires.

He dropped the tongue and picked up the strop. "You're only getting five," he told her. She may want more, and probably would, but he wouldn't give more than she could handle. And in the mindset she'd slipped into, she could think she wanted more than her body could take. He wouldn't allow any harm to come to her.

The first lash of the strop pushed her body forward on the bed. The second flattened her against the mattress. Her ass bounced beneath the force, and dark red blotches were left behind when he pulled back. Third and fourth lashes were received with a low guttural sound. She'd found her bliss, and by the last stroke, she was nearly limp.

He tossed the strop on the bed, and sat beside her. He ran his hand over her ass, feeling the warmth and the raised markings from the tongue, while he also ran his other hand over her head.

"Baby? Color?"

"Yellow, sir." She turned her head, facing him, and he wiped away the hair covering her face. Flushed skin, glazed eyes, and the soft look of solitude. She'd found her quiet place.

He sat beside her, stroking her hair, running fingertips over her ass, watching to be sure she took her breaths and found her way back down to him. His cock wanted attention, wanted to get inside of her, but he wouldn't put his wants ahead of her needs. Not after she just gave every ounce of trust to him.

He got off the bed and went about arranging the covers. "Come on, let's get in bed." He helped her stand up and scooped her off her feet and carried her the three steps to the bed, sliding her beneath the covers.

"Come with me." She snuggled into the pillows and grabbed for him.

He shucked his clothes, stripping down to his boxers, and climbed in with her, pulling her to him and wrapping his arms around her.

His chin rested on her head, and he took a deep breath. As a child, the smell of cookies baking away in the oven reminded him of home. The scent of his mother's perfume gave him the sense of security, but none of those could compare to the richness and the fullness of completion the scent of his girl, his Sydney, gave him.

* * *

HIS BODY WARMED HER. Not in a furnace blowing at full speed sort of warmth, but the sort that fills you with comfort from the inside out. Lying in his arms, feeling all the tingles, and the burn from their playtime, met a need she never admitted even to herself she had. To be comforted. To be taken to a place with his belt, or a whip, to let her mind settle, let her body just feel alive and then eased back into reality with his arms around her, and a soft kiss to the back of her head.

Maybe he thought she was asleep. Her body could probably just fall right into a deep slumber after what he just put it through, but her mind was focused. Not so much on her troubles, but on him. His breathing pattern remained steady, as did the stroke of his hand. His fingertips continued to trail down her arm and then back up again. The man knew how to soothe her, or maybe it was just one of his dom tricks.

Doms had those, right? Little tricks to help a sub after they just flew off into subspace. Sydney knew what subspace was. She'd read about it, heard other women at the club explain it, but until she met Tate, she had never before even come close to experiencing it. Even if she still struggled over being so accepting of her enjoyment of harder play, he was right at home with it.

Based on the thickness of his cock, she figured he enjoyed it every bit as much as she did.

"Tate?" She kept her voice soft, just in case he was starting to doze.

"Yeah?" His hand stilled at her elbow.

"If I was just into a little spanking. You know, like instead of having that whip in my basket, I had just a ping-pong paddle or something, would that change things? Would you still want to play with me?" The question came out of the left field of her mind. She hadn't meant to ask or even broach that subject.

He shifted, rolling her to her back so he could look down at

145

her. A deep crease crossed his forehead.

"I wouldn't do more than you wanted. If you only wanted a spanking, sure we could do that. But I don't think we would have been attracted to each other in the first place if that was the case." He snagged a loose hair from her cheek and pushed it away from her face. His touch gentle and tender, a complete contradiction to the sharpness of the whip or his belt.

"How'd you know I was a little more...well, that I wanted..." She sighed. He'd been so patient with her, the least she could do was finally be open with herself. And him. "That I wanted harsher play than I had at the club?"

A grin crossed his lips. "Anyone who watched you could see that. You don't hide your frustration very well when you aren't getting what you want."

"But the other guys I've played with never seemed to know."

"Because they weren't invested. They didn't watch you other than to play with you one time or maybe two. They were just giving you what you said you wanted. It was a scene to them. That's all."

"But not with you?" If her mouth could just close, that would be great. These deep conversations were best left to Riley. She dealt with feelings a hell of a lot better than Sydney.

Tate laughed. "No. When you didn't have a spot at the roulette game, I made sure I could get a table with you."

"That night didn't go very well, though. You said I was a brat. You said you couldn't handle me." She pointed out while pointing a finger at him.

He captured her finger with his hand. "No. We had this discussion already. That night didn't go well because I could see you wanted more than the little spanking I gave you, but when we talked you kept avoiding it. I mean we talked about our kinks, but you stayed away from admitting to loving hard play, to wanting the pain. Instead you tried to brat your way into a harder spanking. Thinking if I was annoyed, I'd deliver."

"Maybe I just wanted the domestic discipline side of things."
She cocked an eyebrow. It wasn't fair he could read her so well
when she could barely understand herself.

"Maybe. But I think that's just a role-play fantasy for you. You
want to be the naughty wife who gets a bare bottom spanking for
burning the roast. But then you want to be tied up, whipped,
toyed with and fucked hard."

Her cheeks heated and her body reacted to the scene he
described. Pulling the cover up over her face became her new
fantasy.

"So, tell me, Sydney. Did you like the devil's tongue?"

He shifted again, pressing his body against hers.

Time for truth. "Yes. It was better than I thought it would be. It
hurt, but in a really awesome way."

He smiled, little wrinkles formed around his eyes. "And
the strop?"

"The strop was horrible." She grinned. "But it had the right
amount of thud mixed with sting to just send me away. Isn't that
weird? For your mind to just spiral outside yourself. I could feel
what you were doing. I heard the sound of the strop, felt it, but it
didn't register as pain. It just registered as—I don't know how to
describe it—it was just exactly right. You know, exactly right."

He kissed her. His hands dove into her hair, his body moved to
lay over her and his mouth completely captured hers. His tongue
licked at her bottom lip, taking over and thrusting inside of her
mouth. She had no more control over the kiss than she did when
he was whipping her, and the effect was the same.

"How's your ass?" he asked after breaking the kiss, his lips still
hovering close to hers.

"It hurts, but not bad. Just hot."

"How're your legs?"

"If you're asking me if I'm okay, I'm perfect. But I'd be a lot
better if your boxers would disappear."

He chuckled and gave her one hard quick kiss. "I would, too."

147

He pushed her legs apart and knelt between them, making quick work of getting rid of his boxers and freeing his cock. She licked her lips when his hard shaft bobbed before her.

She reached out and wrapped her hand around his cock, smiling at the guttural groan he unleashed.

"Fuck." He didn't stop her, so she began to stroke him, watching his face as she did so. His eyes were on her. Not her hand, but on her and he looked to be a man possessed.

When a small bead of pre-cum appeared, she wiped it with her thumb and brought it to her mouth. Still keeping their eyes locked, she sucked the moisture off the pad of her thumb.

"That's enough teasing." He reached over the side of the bed, dug around a bit in his jeans and when he reappeared he held a condom.

"Let me?" she asked with her palm out.

He narrowed his eyes, but handed the foil packet to her. Scooting back, she sat up and opened the package. She could sense him watching her, which is exactly what she wanted. As she rolled the latex over his thick shaft, she applied pressure with her fingers and again she was gifted with a low growl.

"Spread your legs. Now." He pressed her shoulders down until she lay on the bed.

"I guess the romance is over?" She giggled.

His fingers clamped around her sore nipples. "This is the romance you understand."

She arched her back, presenting her breasts upward for him. "Yes." She nodded and winced when he let go of her.

"Now for this pussy." He hooked his hands under her knees and drew them further apart, looking down at her sex, already wet for him. "Keep your legs open for me, I'm going to fuck this pussy, hard and fast, and you'll take it. You got it?"

Take it? Like it would be some sort of punishment? If he didn't start soon, she was going to take over. Though she knew that wouldn't get her anywhere.

"Yes, sir," she complied. Anything at this point to get his cock inside of her. She'd been slick with need since the moment he'd walked into her apartment, and it had only grown more urgent when he spanked her, the whipping and clothes pins had made her feel as though she were starving.

She wrapped her arms around her knees, pulling her legs up to her chest and his approval shone in his eyes.

He slid his cock through her folds. So damn close.

With him poised at her entrance, she watched his face, basking at how much discipline and control he possessed. His eyes betrayed that control. He wanted inside as much as she wanted him there. Even so, he paused, waiting.

"Tate! Sir! Please!" She wiggled her bottom, the delightful tenderness from the spankings sparking a new lust, a desperate need.

"Beg me." He lowered his face toward her. She could feel the warmth of his breath as he gave his command.

She wasn't above pleading, not now, not when his cock was so close to her. "Please, Tate, sir, please fuck me right now." She may have growled the last part, and it probably came out more of an order than a plea, but he had the good grace to overlook her folly.

With one forceful thrust he was inside her, his balls pressed against her ass, and his cock filling her completely.

She heard her own satisfied cry fill the room.

"Oh, fuck." He pulled back, only to thrust forward again with a savage force, impaling her to the hilt. He was in so deep, filling her so much she could only accept what he gave her. To take what he dished out.

"Tate." Her nails bit into her own thigh, holding her legs open for him, letting him ravage her the way he intended, the way her body craved. Every thrust harder than the one before it. His stare so intense it pinned her to the bed, making her unable to do anything other than obey him, to belong to him.

"This pussy, this body, they're mine now." He pinched a nipple, a little tweak really, but in its sensitive state the sensation heightened.

"Yes, sir." She nodded, it wasn't something she could really deny. Not when her body reacted to him as though he had more power over it than she did.

He ground his hips into her, rubbing her clit and sending her even closer to her climax. "I have to come." She moved her hands to his shoulders, planting her feet on the bed and matching his thrusts.

"Not yet." He shook his head, giving her the devil's grin. "If you do, I'll spank your pussy with the little paddle I saw."

No. Never. She knew which leather paddle he referred to, and no way did she want that near her clit. Not now, not when she was so close.

"Please, Tate! I have to come," she begged.

He plowed faster and harder into her. A claiming. He was taking ownership, not just of her body, but of her. And each thrust of his cock seemed to seal them, bring them closer to a place she didn't think she could be with someone else. Safety. Pleasure filled with acceptance and love.

"You better behave." He rolled his hips, making her clit feel every bit of pressure he applied. "If you don't, what will happen? What happens to my naughty girl?"

If he was trying to see if words could make a girl come, he was getting pretty damn close to success.

"You'll spank me," she answered, feeling her eyes roll back and the pleasure ramp up in her clit.

"How will I spank you? How will my naughty girl be punished?"

The man was set on killing her with denial.

"You'll, oh fuck, you'll make me come, too many times, fuck, and then you'll spank me." She didn't like his punishments. Which was probably the point, but describing them, saying the words out loud nearly undid her.

"Yes, I will. Every time. And what about my good girl?" His own breath became shallow. His thread of control thinned out to match her own.

"You'll let me come! Please Tate! I'm good. I've been good! Please!"

He brought his face right down to hers. His nose brushing against hers. "Come for me, baby. Come hard." He claimed her mouth as his cock claimed her body.

Her body exploded into an orgasm so powerful it felt as though a million shards of herself floated everywhere as his cock continued to ram into her, driving her through the ecstasy. She screamed, but it was lost in his kiss. Every nerve ending of her body came alive, not an inch of her didn't feel her release.

And just as it began to ebb, he thrust harder again, finding his own release. He broke off the kiss to call out his own pleasure. His balls slapped against her ass, and when he stilled, letting the waves of his own orgasm carry him away, she could feel every ounce of his energy pour into her.

Everything was quiet aside from the heaviness of their breathing. Breaths coming and going at the same time, their hearts pounding, chest to chest.

He lifted his head, kissing her and rubbing his nose against hers. She sighed, unable to say or do much else but breathe. After long minutes passed, he pulled out of her, disappearing for several minutes into the bathroom, leaving her cold and empty.

When he returned, his cock at half mast, he jumped back into the bed, yanking the covers over them and pulling her into his arms. "You know what, Sydney?"

"What?" she sighed and snuggled into the safe haven that was his arms.

"I think we can eat that pizza now."

She laughed. The pizza had long ago been forgotten, but at the mention of it, her stomach growled.

"I knew you'd agree," he teased, and patted her belly.

CHAPTER 12

*S*pending the night at Sydney's apartment had left Tate running behind in the morning. He could try to blame her, and had in fact done so as he made his way out the door, but it had been him. His insatiable need to be near her, touching her, fucking her.

He'd never been one for morning sex. Most girls he'd spent the night with were the same way. They might roll out of bed, grab a quick shower and then come back for more loving, but that was as close to morning sex as he'd ever gotten. Not with Sydney. Now that she felt comfortable in asking for what she wanted, she wasn't backing down.

No, that's not true. She didn't exactly ask for the morning fucking he gave her. At least not with words. It was the smile. When she rolled over and opened her eyes, finding him looking at her, she smiled. A gentle little curve to her lips that made creases on the sides. It wasn't just a good morning smile. It was an *I'm so fucking glad you're here* smile. And he couldn't let honesty like that go unrewarded.

"Nice of you to show." John gave a smug grin from the entrance of Overtime. Another BDSM club, pretty popular in the community, but not exclusive like Black Light. Memberships weren't as difficult to obtain and there were a lot of people who only used the club infrequently. All of which might make finding more information on the two victims very difficult.

"Shut it." Tate fell into step with John.

"With the DA again?"

"With Veronica, again?" Tate asked pointing at his shirt. The same one he'd worn the night before. John rarely settled down with one woman for more than two nights in a row. Veronica must have a gift to keep a drifter like John coming around.

"Shut it." John laughed. "You sure anyone will be here? It's the middle of the afternoon."

"Wilkins said he'd be available. I called them this morning."

"Who knew how valuable your sex life would be to this case."

"Just stay out of my sex life." Tate pointed at him.

John nodded. "Fair enough. Now, what do you think we'll find here?"

"I'm hoping to find someone that might lead us to some play partners of the vics. From what I found out, both played here, so there has to be someone who knows something."

Tate pulled open the door to the club, an old warehouse turned into a kinky funhouse, and waved John in.

"Tate!" Wilkins, one of the owners, greeted them. "It's been a while."

"Uh, yeah." Tate shook his hand, but didn't elaborate.

"Oh, don't get all red in the face. Black Light's taken some of our regulars, but we aren't hurting. There's plenty of kinksters that need a reasonable membership fee and don't require the anonymity Black Light offers."

"True. This is my partner, John. I mentioned him on the phone."

"Yes, yes. Here, let's go in my office." He led them around the front entrance to his office. If Tate wasn't misreading John, he seemed a little disappointed not to be walking through the dungeon.

"So. You had some questions about some girls." Wilkins sat behind his desk, and leaned forward on his forearms.

"Yes, these." John handed him the pictures of the two victims.

"We've been told they were seen playing here before, and we were hoping you'd be able to point us in the direction of some of their play partners. Maybe a boyfriend or Dom of one of the girls? We haven't been able to find anything suggesting they had any romantic involvements."

"Yeah, you wouldn't." Wilkins flipped through the photos, plucking one out and tossing it on the desk. "Cheryl has a very conservative family. If she was dating a guy from the club, she didn't bring him home to meet Mommy and Daddy."

"Did you see her playing with guys here in the club?" John asked.

"No, not really. These two were friends, they were always together when I saw them. But this one didn't play, at least not very often. I do remember one guy, though. Short scene. Real short. A few slaps on her ass, and the guy started digging out his cock. A real newb."

"I guess she didn't want to play along then?" John asked.

Wilkins laughed. "No. Not many would. Kind of a jerk move, even for a sex club." He looked at the other two photos. "I don't know if this other one played with him, but I do remember there being some sort of argument between them. It was after the bad scene with her friend. Daryl, one of the DMs for the night, broke it up, sent him packing for the night, and I think he suspended his membership for a period of time. I'll have to check, though, to be sure."

"What's this winner's name?" Tate asked.

"Goes by The Dom. My computer's all jammed up with a virus, the IT guy's coming this afternoon to fix it. Once I can get in it, I can get you his real name."

"The Dom?" Tate raised an eyebrow.

"Yeah, real ego trip, that guy." Wilkins nodded.

"Think we can talk with Daryl about the argument?" John asked, scribbling in his note pad.

"Yeah, sure. I'll text you his info." Wilkins took out his phone and tapped away after Tate gave him the number.

Tate checked the message that came through and nodded. "Thanks, we'll give him a call."

* * *

"I'M TELLING you this is a horrible idea." Riley shuffled down the tunnel behind Sydney, still trying to convince her to go back to the car. "You are going to get us both in trouble."

Sydney spun around, nearly getting knocked to the ground when Riley ran into her. "First of all, you don't have to be here. You can go back up to the car at any moment. So, if you aren't supposed to be here and you get in trouble, that's on you. Besides, it's Dane. That man loves you too much to really punish you."

"I think I can safely say that's not the case." Riley shook her head. "But what's the second of all?"

"What?"

"You said first of all, what's the second of all?"

"Oh. Second of all, why would we get into trouble? Black Light is safe, and besides Tate's not going to be mad." She'd told herself all day long he wouldn't be, hoping to convince herself. Working with the notion that since she'd given in and started to accept what she liked, things were comfortable. And yet, a small part of her still felt a little tingle in her chest that signaled she was doing something wrong — something he wouldn't like.

"I remember you telling me he said you couldn't come to Black Light without him," Riley pointed out.

"That was before. Now, we know each other a bit better, I'm sure it's fine." Sydney started walking again through the underground tunnel that would take them to the entrance to the club. Overthinking her decision wouldn't help, and besides, they were already at the club.

"You're so sure about that you didn't tell him where you were going tonight." Riley's whispered comeback was heard and ignored. She'd told him she was having a girl's night out. He didn't ask questions, just said to have a good time. And she would.

"Hey, Sydney. Riley." Danny greeted them once they made it into the entrance. "One locker or two?"

"Just one is fine." Riley slid her purse off her shoulder and waited for a locker to pop open for her to stuff her things into. Sydney tossed her wallet inside along with her cell phone and handed Danny her membership card.

"Are Tate and Dane with you girls?" he asked, looking back at the entrance.

"Uh, no." Riley answered giving Sydney one more glare before handing over the cards. "Dane had a meeting tonight."

"And Tate?" Danny eyed Sydney.

"Busy." She nodded and took her card back from him after he held it under the black light to find the membership logo.

"Well, have fun." Danny looked no more convinced by Sydney than Riley did, but she wasn't going to think about it. If Tate was angry she would just explain she wanted a night of relaxation and sitting in a crowded bar with loud music and gyrating twenty somethings did not give her that. Hanging at Black Light and watching the scenes, having some girl talk with her friend, that was girl's night. The little tingle in her chest intensified with every attempt to convince herself she wasn't directly disobeying him.

Sydney walked through the door into the dungeon and took a deep breath. Already, play was in full swing. She could smell the leather, the sweat, the sex. Intoxicating. Home.

"Let's get a drink." She walked over to the bar and ordered a glass of wine. Since she had no intention of playing with anyone, she could give over to some libations with no guilt.

"Okay, so catch me up on the case you're working on with Tate." Riley sat across from her with her Diet Coke.

"I may not get to do much else with it. Since Michael Stanley signed that bogus confession, Vargas doesn't want me to do anything else except get ready for a sentencing hearing." The conversation hadn't gone well, and had ruined her entire afternoon.

"Well, how do you know it's bogus? Maybe he actually did it."

"No. No way. He has no connection to the girls. Someone's making him confess. There's more to it. I know it."

"Hey! Sydney!" The chair beside her scraped the floor as it was yanked back and a man plopped down in it. Dominick.

She internally groaned. He didn't know how to take a kindly brush off. He wasn't the most inexperienced dom she'd ever played with, but he definitely had the quickest draw.

"Dominick. Hi." She forced a smile. "This is my good friend, Riley."

Dominick nodded at Riley but then turned to Sydney. "You want to go another round tonight? My dance card is pretty empty."

She managed not to snort. Dance card? A man who could barely get through a warm up spanking without pulling out his cock wasn't exactly in hot demand.

"Um, I can't. Thanks though."

His casual smile dropped. "Why not?"

Startled at first by the blunt question, she recovered enough to keep from scowling. "I'm involved with someone, and we don't play with other people."

"Involved? With who? That guy who finger banged you after I got you all horny?"

Was this guy serious? Even Riley, who had a much higher tolerance for jackasses, was staring at him with disgust.

"Tate and I are together now, so I can't play with you tonight." She decided not to point out that he hadn't done anything to get her hot and bothered. She'd barely felt the spanking he gave, and as soon as she realized his zipper was coming down, she'd jumped off the bench.

"Fine." He looked over at Riley. "What about you?"

"Sorry, Dominick. Both ladies are spoken for." A deep voice reverberated behind Sydney.

Of course. She really should have known.

Dominick didn't even bother with a civil reply, he just stood up and walked away shaking his head.

"I thought you had a meeting." Riley stood up and opened her arms for a hug.

Dane kissed her and gave her ass a squeeze. "And I thought *you* were having a girl's night out."

"We are." Riley said. "See, girls, and we're out."

"Uh huh."

"What are you doing here anyway?" Sydney all but hissed.

Dane laughed and took Dominick's vacated seat. "Calm down, I'm not going to ruin your fun. I was driving home, and I noticed Riley's car. I tried calling, but you must have already been inside."

"I didn't think you'd mind."

Dane patted Riley's arm. "I don't. I wish you would have said this was where you were going, but I don't mind if you hang out here."

"See." Sydney pointed at Dane. "I told you it was fine."

"Maybe for me, but I'm not thinking it's the same for you." Riley gave her a crooked smile.

"If it's fine for you, it's fine for me." Sydney sipped her wine.

"By chance, did Tate specifically tell you that you weren't allowed to come here without him?" Dane asked, leaning closer to her with one of his annoyingly cute smiles.

"Well, yeah, but things are different now."

"In what way?" Dane asked.

"Sydney." Riley started to speak but Dane pointed a finger at her, silencing her.

"Well, things have gotten a little more serious."

"And you think that means rules are less important?" Dane asked, reaffirming his pointed finger at Riley to keep her quiet.

Sydney rolled her eyes. "Not less important, but less necessary."

"I wonder what Tate would think about that." Dane sat back in his chair.

"Happy to answer that for you." Tate's voice startled Sydney.

With a forced calm, she downed her glass of wine, placed the glass on the table and scooted her chair back. Standing up, she smoothed out the skirt of her dress and turned around to face Tate.

"Hi." Not exactly what she'd been ready to say, but she hadn't counted on his dark expression.

"Hi." He nodded and looked past her to Dane and Riley. "She's going to be busy tonight, so I'm guessing the girl's night is over."

"Yeah. I think so." Riley had a little more amusement in her voice than Sydney could forgive. They were supposed to stick together, weren't they?

"Tate, I told you I was having a night out with Riley. What are you doing here?"

"I came by to ask Jaxson another question. What exactly are you doing here?" He folded his arms over his chest, as though he needed anything else to add to his already formidable stance.

"Oh, what do you need to ask him?" Focusing on the case might at least smooth out the fierce wrinkle in his forehead.

"I already did."

"Okay, and what was it?" She took a small step back, hitting the table with her ass. The wine glass wobbled.

"First, I think you should answer my question. What are you doing here?"

"Relaxing. Having a glass of wine with my friend. Like I said I was doing." What could he have needed to ask Jaxson that would require him to stop at the club and not just give him a call. "Did you really need to ask Jaxson something or did you track me down?"

"And are you supposed to be here without me?" His eyes darkened, if that were even possible considering how dangerous he'd already looked.

"Here, like in Washington D.C.?" Even she could admit that was lame, but he hadn't answered her question so she could forgive herself for some delay in answering his.

"Oh, Sydney." Riley whispered her plea.

"Since your girl's night is canceled, how about we go get some dinner. Then you can explain all about why you neglected to tell me the location of your girl's night," Dane said to Riley.

"You said you weren't upset." Riley pointed out.

Sydney watched Tate, who watched her right back.

"I'm not, but still, it's a conversation worth having. Good luck, Syd." Dane patted her shoulder and escorted his girlfriend to the exit.

"She's my ride," Sydney whispered.

"Oh, I think I can manage to get you home." Tate nodded. "What I'm deciding on is should I punish you here, or when we get home?"

"Punish? Tate. There's no reason to punish me."

"Right. Home it is."

She found herself being hauled out of the club and back to Danny, who happily opened the locker for her with a smug grin. As she followed Tate back toward the tunnel, she heard him chuckling. She'd have to wait until the next time she saw him to give him a talking to. Tate didn't seem to be in the frame of mind for her to do so at the moment.

CHAPTER 13

*T*he man who murdered those girls had a definite tie to the clubs. Tate couldn't prove it, not yet, but he knew it. The murderer found the girls at a club and used their kink as a way to get them bound, so he could do the unspeakable to them.

Sydney had been the one to convince him Michael Stanley wasn't the real killer, and yet there she was gallivanting around at Black Light as though the real one wasn't out loose in the city.

"Tate, I know you're upset, but I don't think you need to be."

Not exactly the words he wanted to hear from the woman standing buck ass naked in the corner of his bedroom. At least she had the smarts not to turn around again to try and talk with him. The large red hand print on her left cheek obviously left a mark on more than her skin.

"Sydney, were you told not to go the club without me?" He crossed his ankles and his arms.

"Yes, but—"

"And, did you discuss with me changing that rule before you went and broke it?"

"Well, no, but—"

"Then I want your mouth shut. Not another word until your

punishment is over, and then you'll get to speak. And if you can't do it on your own, I have my ball gag right over here, ready to step in." He picked up the gag he had next to him and waved it around. Even if she couldn't see it, she could hear the jangling of the buckles.

"This isn't exactly what I had in mind when I told you I had domestic discipline fantasies," she muttered into the corner. Her ass clenched, perhaps expecting another smack for her back talk.

Since she couldn't see him, he gave in to the tug of a smile. She sounded downright pathetic standing in the corner. She may have fantasies of being spanked like a naughty wife, but when it came time to take actual discipline, she was just miserable.

"One more word and I put in the gag." He thumbed the red ball. Just imagining the ball in her mouth made his cock hard. He hoped she could keep her mouth shut, if he used the gag, he might not be able to administer her full punishment. His body was addicted to hers, but she needed to know that every time she crossed that line, he'd be there to push her back.

"Come here." He called a few minutes later. She turned around and shuffled her feet across the carpeting until she got to him. Her arms were folded over her stomach, pushing up her breasts toward him. "I want you to go in that drawer and get me the paddle and the vibrator. Then you're going to come over here and lay on the floor, on your back, your legs spread wide."

Her forehead creased, and her eyes darted to the nightstand.

"Now, Sydney. You don't want to add any more to what you have coming. The marks from the other night have faded, but I'm sure you're still a little tender."

She gave a little nod and went into action. When she returned, she handed him the wooden hairbrush-shaped paddle and held out the white bullet vibrator.

"No, you keep that. Now on your back."

She gave him a worried look, but moved to the floor.

"Legs." He pushed her knees apart with his boot. "Good. Now."

He leaned forward, resting his elbows on his knees. "Fuck your-self. Two orgasms, then we'll get to the spanking."

"Tate." She groaned.

"Did you want me to make it three?"

"No, sir."

With a twist of the base, the vibrator came to life. He tried to look at the scene before him clinically. Just something that needed doing, except even with her disgruntled look, she was beyond gorgeous. Submitting to his authority, accepting her punishment, nothing could be more beautiful in that moment.

Her first orgasm came quickly. Standing in the corner for twenty minutes contemplating the spanking coming to her, prob-ably had her on edge. The second would take longer, she didn't enjoy multiple orgasms. Which only made them all the more necessary.

"Come like a good girl, Sydney." He said as he kicked off his boots and pulled his socks free. "Give me another orgasm. You can do this."

She groaned. "I can't!" But she didn't turn off the vibrator.

"You can, and you don't have a choice. You're being punished for being naughty. So, make yourself come." He ran his bare foot down her leg and then back up again.

She closed her eyes and bucked up at the vibrator.

"You were a bad girl, now you have to come like one. Come for me."

She bit down hard on her lower lip and her hips began to move with her vibrator. Her sex was wet, filling the room with the scent of her arousal.

"Sydney." He put some warning in his tone.

"Fuck!" She screamed and her eyes flew open as her orgasm tore through her. She tossed the vibrator to the side and sucked in air.

The second was never as much fun as the first, and he bet it was almost painful. When she calmed her breathing, and looked at him, the arousal he'd seen earlier was gone.

"Perfect." He held out his hand to help her up from the floor. "Put the vibrator on the nightstand, you can clean it later."

She swallowed and did as he instructed.

He settled on the bed, picking up the paddle. "Get the chair in the corner and bring it here."

She huffed but complied all the same. Once the chair was where he directed, he told her to put her hands flat on the cushion.

"Not over your lap?" she asked, with a little more sadness than he could stand. He wanted her contrite, remorseful, but he didn't like her sad.

"You didn't think following my rules was worthy of your attention tonight. So no, you won't get the comfort of my lap. Now, hands flat and stick that ass out."

Once she was in position he stood beside her, wrapping his arm around her waist. She would wiggle and jump, no way to avoid that with the wooden paddle, but she wouldn't get away.

"I hope you have a real soft chair at work, you're going to need it tomorrow." Those were the last words he spoke before bringing down the paddle on her perfectly shaped ass. He delivered three sharp slaps to her naked globes. The sound filled the room and her squeal corresponded perfectly with his rhythm. Alternating between cheeks, he covered her entire backside, bringing it to a nice rosy color.

She began to hop from foot to foot, but he held onto her waist tightly as he began the last round. "When I give a rule, there's a reason. This one was for your safety, and you just figured you didn't need to follow it. Well, now you'll remember every time you sit tomorrow how important your safety is to me." He brought the little paddle down hard on the up-curve of her ass, eliciting a howl of protest from her.

"Disregarding the rules is bullshit. I won't tolerate it, and you don't want me to," Another hard blow on her other cheek. She stomped a foot. He could hear the sniffles between strikes.

"I'm sorry, Tate!" She tried to stand up after a particularly harsh strike to her thigh.

He got her back in position. "Three more," he responded.

"Please!" Her hand flew back, but he caught it and held it to her side.

"Did you want me to make it five?"

"No!" She shook her head.

"Then take your spanking like a good girl." Without giving her more time to argue or make her situation worse for herself, he delivered the last three strokes, quickly and firmly to her sit spots. By the time he finished, she was dancing from foot to foot and full on crying.

He tossed the damn paddle to the floor and gathered her in his arms. She gripped his shirt in her fists and cried into it.

"I hate that paddle. I hate you making me come like that."

"I hate when you disobey, and I have to do those things," he countered, wiping the tears from her reddened face.

"I hate that, too." She whispered and buried her face back into his shirt.

* * *

SYDNEY STARED at the reflection of her ass in Tate's full-length bathroom mirror. She'd pegged her ass to be black and blue by morning, but nothing. A tiny little mark on one cheek, That could just as easily have been from him pinching her ass than the spanking he gave her.

She could smell coffee brewing from the kitchen, and hear him wrestling pans to make breakfast. She had told him not to bother, but he insisted. A good breakfast to start the day off right. She'd thought the mind-altering sex they just experienced in the shower was a better way to start the day, but she supposed some pancakes would be good, too.

By the time she dressed, breakfast was already being plated up.

"What time do you need to get to the office?" he asked, looking at the clock on the microwave.

"I'm not sure I should even bother. Vargas, my boss, won't let me pursue the case anymore. He said I have to get ready for the sentencing hearing for Mr. Stanley, not be an investigator in a closed case." She rolled her eyes and took her seat at the kitchen island where a plate of fluffy pancakes and a hot cup of coffee were waiting for her.

"Well, you can do that while John and I keep investigating. Our chief hasn't stopped us, and after John told him what we found out yesterday, he gave the green light to keep it open."

"What did you find out?" They'd only had a brief conversation the day before. She had thought it would be better not to overindulge in talking with him since she hadn't wanted to tell him about heading to Black Light after work. Turned out, her plan hadn't helped her at all.

He smiled. "We went to Overtime and talked with Wilkins, the owner. He said the girls both went there, together most times, and they had some sort of run in with one of the Doms. He's getting me the guy's real name and contact information."

"Why didn't you tell me you were going there? I could have gone with." She might have other questions to ask. If Stanley was innocent, she needed to know so she could stop her department from going forward with the sentencing hearing. Didn't he understand how important it was to make sure the guy was guilty? Why would he leave her out of the interview with the club owner, unless he figured she'd just make trouble.

"You were in the office. You know, you have other cases besides this one, and you just said your boss doesn't want you investigating Stanley anymore."

"This one is a priority." She planted her hands on the island.

"Why is this one such a priority? I mean, I understand your ethics and morals; you want to be sure you're putting away an actual guilty person. But not one DA—or assistant DA—I've ever worked with has been this determined."

Her heat sank into her stomach. She wouldn't go down that road with him. Not with anyone. Things in the past needed to stay buried there. Another of her mother's motto's, and one of the few she agreed with.

"Well, I'm not other DAs," she said, her voice thickening.

"Yes, that's for sure, I wouldn't paddle any of the others. Even though I'm sure most of them deserve it." He cracked another smile, but she was past the humor.

"So, let me get this straight. I don't tell you I'm going to Black Light, I get punished. You don't tell me a big part of a case we are both working on, and what? Nothing?"

He pushed away from the counter he was leaning against. The smile vanished from his lips, and the crease in his brow deepened. "Yes, let's get this straight for you. You broke a rule. You weren't supposed to go to Black Light or any other club without me. And you did. The reason you didn't tell me was because you were breaking that rule. So yes, you got punished. And if you don't correct your tone, it could be happening again before you go to work."

"But you can go investigating without me, and I'm not allowed to get upset?" Detract and deflect, her own personal favorite motto.

His jaw clenched and released. "I was doing my job, you know, as the lead detective on the case? You were doing your job, as the prosecuting attorney by being in your office working."

She stared at him, hard. Her job was to put the bad guys behind bars. *Only* the bad guys. Why wouldn't he understand that she needed to be sure, especially when so much about the case made little sense?

There wasn't time to argue, that's what she told herself as she felt the urgency in her chest build. He wouldn't understand, or he couldn't. Either way, talking about it would only bring up old memories she'd done her best to keep buried.

"Your rule is stupid. Michael Stanley is locked up for crimes I'm sure he didn't commit. So why the hell would the real killer go off and commit another murder? Wouldn't that sort of ruin his plan of framing the wrong guy? And besides, I was at Black Light. Do you know how much fucking security they have there? I'm safer there than my apartment!"

"The killer is a Dominant. I'm positive of that."

"Again, if the guy he's framing is awaiting trial, we have at least that long until he strikes again," she said.

The tension in his body didn't ease with her logic. If anything, he tensed more.

"It doesn't matter. I told you, you aren't to go to the club without me."

"And it's a stupid rule," she yelled at him. Well, in for a penny and all that, she supposed.

His eyes widened when her voice rose, but he was even more shock stricken when she pushed herself out of the chair, letting it fly back to the floor and stomped out of the kitchen.

"Sydney!" He caught up to her in the living room. "I get you don't agree with it, but it's the rule, and I'm not changing it."

"Yeah, well, I'm not following it," she snapped at him.

"You're doing it again. You're upset about something else and instead of dealing with it, you're just gonna fly off the handle and hide!" he said.

The familiar panic rose up in her chest. The same sensation she always got when it was too much, when the feelings she covered up rose too close to the surface, threatening to be exposed. She needed to get away before he drudged it all up again.

"You're not going to follow that rule, or any of my rules?" he questioned in a low voice, much lower than she'd heard him use before.

"Well, that one in particular." She stood firm, fisting her hands at her sides.

He wiped his face with his hand.

"Then I don't get how this is supposed to work. How does it work, Sydney, if you get to decide which rules you follow and which you don't?" If she had seen anger in his eyes, or heard it in his voice, it would have been easier for her to take the question. But there wasn't anger. Only exasperation and tiredness. He was giving up. She'd pushed him too far.

Well. Fine.

"I guess it doesn't." She turned and disappeared back into the bedroom to get her shoes and purse. Tate didn't follow her, not that she expected him to. He wasn't the chase the girl down sort of guy.

"Sydney." He tried to talk to her as she walked past him in the living room, but she just threw up her middle finger and stalked for the front door. "You are going to regret your behavior," he warned.

Tears burned her eyes, but she wouldn't, couldn't, let him see them. She yanked the front door open and slammed it shut behind her. Pounding the elevator button with the heel of her hand she felt the first tear fall down her cheek.

Well, another one bites the dust. She jumped into the elevator and slammed her hand into the lobby button. *You're going to regret your behavior.* She already did.

CHAPTER 14

*T*wo days. Forty-eight hours since Sydney stormed out of his condo, and still Tate had no idea what the fuck happened. Everything spiraled out of his grasp so quickly, he never had a chance to catch it, and even now, days later, he still couldn't make heads or tails of the conversation.

One minute they were about to sit down for breakfast, the next she was storming out. He'd seen temper tantrums before. No matter how old or how mature, he'd never known a submissive that didn't have at least one during their relationship, and almost always they were stress related.

That could be the case. It could be because they were getting closer to each other.

Closer. That didn't even begin to describe it for him. Every day began with Sydney on his mind, and every night ended with her in his last thoughts before drifting off to sleep.

He'd loved women before, felt strong feelings for them, but nothing compared to this. This was like living in hell and heaven at the same time. Every touch scorched him, every smile soothed it away. Sydney was a woman of contradictions, and more than once he'd wanted to yank out his own hair while trying to understand her. But he'd gladly lose every strand on his head if he could understand this last bit.

Wilkins hadn't gotten back to him yet. Some IT glitch had locked down the files with membership information. Without that name, the case was going stale. No new evidence to point to anyone other than Stanley, and what evidence they did have was shitty at best.

If only the man hadn't signed that fucking confession. His attorney kept him away from any police questioning. The files had come over from the gym, and Sydney had been right on the money. Not once was the suspect ever at the gym at the same time as the girls. Not even the same day. Unless he was stalking the gym, Tate couldn't see how Michael Stanley would have even met the girls.

The girls seemed to hang out together in only two locations. The gym and Overtime. Tate had revisited one of the victim's family, hoping to find out something new. So far nothing. They had no idea Jamie was friends with the other victim, Cheryl, and they had no clue what Overtime was.

Her parents had admitted to not seeing very much of their daughter after she graduated college. Apparently, Jamie had gotten a job at an accounting firm and only called home once a week, sometimes every other week. Not wanting to crowd their only daughter, they had let her spread her wings without question.

Of course, now they regretted that action. It wasn't an unhappy family, she still seemed close with her parents, but they, as any victim's family would, wanted more time, and wished they'd made sure she came home to visit more.

Wanting more time, he could understand.

Tate looked at his phone once more, hoping for something, anything, from Sydney. The last message he'd sent her hadn't even been read. She was completely blocking him out.

"Detective Tate?" An older man entered his office.

Tate stood up and greeted him. "Yes, sir. Mr. Florence?"

"Yes. Uh, my wife wouldn't come." Cheryl's father stood clutching his jacket, knuckles nearly white from the strength of his grip.

"I understand. This is very difficult." He gestured toward a chair and walked around the desk and sat down.

"I guess we're a little confused. I understand detective Steinbeck had some medical issues, so you stepped in on the case, but from what we were told, the man he arrested has confessed."

Tate leaned forward. "Yes, sir, he has. We are just trying to tie up any loose ends, make sure the case is solid."

"You don't think he did it." The wrinkles around the man's eyes deepened along with his frown.

"I have some doubts, yes." Being dishonest with the victim's family could only make their pain worse, and although Tate didn't have any children, he'd seen enough during his police career to know what that pain looked like.

"What sort of doubts?"

"I know you said your daughter didn't have any connection to the other girl in this case. I wonder if maybe you have any other information about that? Did maybe she mention the other girl in passing?"

He scratched his head. "No. Not that I recall, but Cheryl didn't talk much about her comings and goings. She always felt her mother and I were a little too conservative. That we wouldn't approve of what she was doing." A sadness tinged his words. "It wasn't true, though. At least I don't think it was. When she was younger she liked to party a little too much, and we did put a stop to that. But she had just started college at the time, it was different. She grew up to be a wonderful woman, independent and strong. I can't imagine she'd be involved in anything we would be so disapproving of."

"Did she ever mention a club named Overtime? Maybe a boy she dated or something like that?"

"Dated? No. She did mention Overtime once. In a phone conversation with someone else. I assumed she was talking about work. It's a club you said?"

"Yes. We've found the connection between your daughter and the other victim. They were friends, but apparently, they only got together at the gym and the club. I hoped maybe she had mentioned something to you or your wife about a man she dated, or someone who was maybe harassing her?"

"No, nothing like that."

"Your wife told Detective Trainer your daughter was supposed to meet her for lunch the day she disappeared," Tate prompted.

"Yes. She was going to the gym before meeting my wife, but she never showed up at the restaurant." Mr. Florence played with the button on his jacket.

"That was unusual?"

"Yes, if she was running late she would have called. To not show up at all worried my wife. She stopped at her apartment on her way home, but she wasn't there either."

"Her door was locked." Tate looked down at the notes from the original conversation with the Florences. "Nothing seemed out of place?"

"My wife didn't have her key with her, so she never went inside. The door was locked, yes."

Tate made more notes in the file.

"You'll find this man. If it's not the one you have in custody, you'll find the right one?"

"We are doing everything we can." Tate put his pen down and stood up. Mr. Florence looked like he wanted more answers. And shouldn't he? It was his daughter, his only child, that had been slaughtered. But telling him what sort of club Overtime was and the specifics of his daughter's death wouldn't bring her back, or bring him any peace. "Thank you for stopping in."

"I wish I had more to say, more information. Cheryl was just so private, even with us. It was like she never thought the world would accept her or something. I wish I'd pressured her more to be open with us, asked more questions and really listened to the answers. She was our only child, and we had her later in life." He dragged his hand through his nearly white hair. "Maybe she thought we were just too old to understand her. Maybe if she'd confided in us more, we'd be able to help find this man. Or we could have helped her not be found by him in the first place."

Tate shook his head and assured him again he would do everything he could to get justice for his daughter. John and Steinbeck had never addressed how the girls were taken or the time line of their disappearances. They had been found in the same place, but their deaths hadn't been simultaneous. It was thought the killer had picked them up individually. But what if they had been picked up at the same time, and he had just taken his time getting around to his sick plan.

He grabbed the medical reports again and headed down to forensics.

* * *

MICHAEL STANLEY SAT at the metal table in a small room at the prison. Sydney stood outside the room, watching him through the two-way mirror.

"Are you sure you want to do this?" Silvia Johnson, Michael's attorney, asked her for the third time.

"Of course, I am." Sydney rolled her shoulders back and took a deep breath. She wasn't sure at all. If she was wrong, if her hunch was off base, she could blow the whole thing. She could lose her job. It was partly for that reason she hadn't informed John or Tate what she was up to. They would have insisted on being there, on wanting to hear everything the man in custody would say, and she needed to do this on her own. John would probably prompt Mr. Stanley to continue his crap confession and Tate would probably be overly protective. If he still had any protective sort of feelings left. Either way, it wouldn't be helpful and she didn't need a bunch of detectives looking over her shoulder while she did her job.

Silvia sighed. "You're not ready, but you'll do it anyway."

Having her old classmate as opposing council hadn't been a concern to Sydney when she had found out. She'd gone up against her before over the years, but it did come in handy when she needed the sort of favor she did regarding Mr. Stanley.

"He signed the confession. Most DAs would take that gift and run."

Sydney glanced over at her. "I'm not most DAs."

"I know." Silvia rested her hand on Sydney's shoulder. "But you can't change what happened twenty years ago, Syd. I know this case may feel similar, but it's not the same."

"I know this guy isn't the guy." Sydney pointed at the beaten down man sitting at the table. His unwashed hair stood up at sporadic places, the dark rings under his eyes indicating he didn't sleep well. Not from guilt. That much Sydney knew, and if she put him in jail for the rest of his life and he was innocent, she'd look the same way soon enough.

"I know I can't fix what happened in the past, but I can do my damnedest to be sure it never happens again." With renewed strength, she readied herself to meet with Mr. Stanley.

She nodded to the guard, who opened the door for her, allowing her entrance.

Dressed in an orange jump suit, one wrist cuffed to the metal bar of the table, Michael Stanley didn't look dangerous. He had some priors on his record, drug charges, but nothing to warrant any fear. The look in his eyes, though, when she walked through the door, showed her he was terrified.

"Mr. Stanley, my name is Sydney Richards. I'm the assistant district attorney who is going to be overseeing your sentencing hearing. Are you sure you don't want your attorney present?"

He leaned back in his chair, running his tongue over his teeth.

She'd let him take control of the room, it would only help her case for him to feel in charge. "No, I don't need her."

"I know you signed a confession. That's why I'm here."

"What, did I not sign it in the right place?" He shifted in his seat.

"No, no you signed in the right spot." She eased back in her chair. A relaxed approach would get her further. "I just, well, something's eating at me. You see, I looked in on your girlfriend."

"Ex-girlfriend," he snapped, but his eyes didn't tell the story of man who disliked his former girlfriend.

"Right. Ex-girlfriend. I looked in on her, I wanted to verify something. Did you know she's pregnant?"

"Yeah? So?" His shoulders rolled back, and his jaw tensed.

"About five months or so, I'd say." A little fact John had left out of the files.

"So? What's her being knocked up have to do with me?" The forced carelessness in his voice contradicted the fists on the table.

"Nothing. I mean, if you're not the father." She drummed her fingers on the tabletop.

"What's this got to do with my confession or those girls I killed?" Apparently detract and distract was his motto as well.

"Well, you see, that's what I need you to clear up for me. I don't see your motive. I need you to tell me why you went after those two girls. What did they do that deserved what you did to them?"

He fidgeted in his seat. "They deserved it. Rich uppity types."

Sydney nearly smiled, but she kept herself under control.

"So, you picked them up at their gym, the one on Bunker Street?"

"Yeah." He nodded.

She should have gone to the prison sooner. When she'd seen Silvia's name on the file two days ago, she should have called her up right then instead of waiting.

"It must have been hard to get both of them in your car unwillingly."

"No, they... I mean I grabbed one then went back another day for another." True, the girls had a different time of death, separated by a day each.

"Huh. And it was the gym on Bunker Street?"

"Yeah. What's this got to do with my girlfriend or the sentencing hearing?" He sat forward, his eyes flicking to the mirror.

"Your ex-girlfriend," she pointed out.

"Yeah, whatever, my ex." He rolled his eyes, but she could see the worry in them.

"Who's pregnant with your baby, and who isn't really your ex. But you're trying to keep her safe, aren't you?" He didn't respond, but his body became rigid. "Someone is pinning this on you and making you take the rap. He threatened your family? Your girlfriend?" History repeated itself over and over again, and right before her eyes she saw her own history.

"Look, I confessed. Just lock me up already." His eyes narrowed to angry slits.

"Except you didn't commit the murders. You didn't pick them up in front of the gym on Bunker Street, because there is no gym on Bunker Street."

"So, I got the street name wrong." He shrugged.

"Did you know that you actually do belong to the same gym as them?"

His mouth dropped open, and his eyes flew to the mirror.

"I think Silvia should come in here now."

"Sure." Sydney waved to the window. "And you said your motive was because they were rich girls who had it coming?"

The door opened and Silvia walked in, stepping behind her client but not offering any advice.

"Yeah."

"Except, Michael, the girls, both of them, had just graduated last year. They both had entry level jobs at different offices. Only one of them had family that was well off, and she was completely independent from them. They weren't rich girls deserving to be killed. They were innocent girls, who pissed someone off. But it wasn't you."

"I said it was!" He jumped up from his chair, but Silvia's hand on his shoulder settled him back down. The guard threw the door open, but Sydney waved him away. The man wasn't dangerous; he was scared for his family.

"Were you a boy scout?" Sydney leaned back in her chair, keeping her tone even.

"What? No."

"Play with bondage?"

"No!"

She could forgive the look of disgust that crossed his face. He obviously didn't know how good it felt to be bound by the right person.

"Hmm." She opened her briefcase and pulled out a bundle of hemp rope she'd borrowed from her personal stash. She'd bought it shortly after meeting Tate, but she put that name out of her head. She couldn't get her heart involved right now, she had to concentrate. "Show me the knots you used on the girls. Here you can use my arms." She unraveled the rope and piled it in front of him and put her wrists together, offering them to him.

He looked at the rope, panic filling his expression.

"Those girls were tied up with a Shibari technique. Not well, but Shibari all the same. So, if it was you, show me."

"I'm not doing this shit!" He thrust the rope back at her. "Are you going to do something?" he snapped at Silvia.

"You want me to stop the prosecution from proving your innocence?" she asked pointing a finger and raising an eyebrow.

His face reddened. "You don't understand."

"Oh, I do." Sydney reached across the table and covered his fist with her hand. "I do understand. You somehow got mixed up with someone who has something over you, and now you're being made to take the fall for his crime. He's threatened your girlfriend, your baby, and you'd do anything to keep them safe. Even go to jail for this crime you did not commit." Sacrifice like that she understood. But she also understood the effect it would have at home even more. "You don't want your little girl or boy to grow up missing you, wishing you were there for their birthday parties, for their dance recitals. You don't want that."

"I want my baby alive!" he yelled.

"We can protect your girlfriend. And you. And the baby," Sydney assured him.

"What, witness protection? Spend the rest of our lives running?"

"There are different situations for different cases, but we can't begin to help if you don't let us, Michael. Your girlfriend will be picked up tonight and put into protective custody if you'll just tell us what we need to know, who we need to find. Because if he did this to these two girls, he'll do it again. He'll keep doing it until we stop him. And you don't want that on your conscience. Because what if he doesn't keep his word? What if he goes after your girlfriend anyway?"

"He wouldn't. Then I'd tell." He raised his chin. Had her father been as naïve as this man sitting in front of her?

"Yeah, but she'd still be dead." Sydney squeezed his hand. "You don't want that any more than I do."

He looked at her for a long moment. The room filled with anxiety and stress. Her heart hammered in her chest, and her toes hurt from curling so tightly in her shoes.

His nostrils flared, and he chewed on his lips. "Fine." He nodded. "I'll tell you what you want, but you get my girl protected first. Like right now."

Sydney nodded. "I'll make the call."

ate knocked on Dane's door. After he rang the bell. Twice.

The door flew open with a disgruntled Dane standing in the doorway.

"Is she here?" Tate demanded. Two days and nights were too damn long to go without at least acknowledging his fucking text messages. He'd gone past the point of irritated at her behavior, to seriously wanting to scream at her. She would learn running away didn't work with him, and ignoring him just because she got a bee up her ass didn't work either.

"Who?"

"Who do you think? Sydney!" Tate took a deep breath. Yelling in the hallway wasn't going to get him anywhere. "I've been trying to get a hold of her. She's not in the office, she's not at home, and she isn't answering my calls."

"Who?" Riley peeked her head around the doorway. "Oh, Sydney."

"Do you know where she is?" Dane looked down at Riley.

"I haven't heard from her." She shrugged. "Is everything okay?

Come in." She gave Dane a little shove to get him out of the way and waved Tate in.

"We had a little disagreement."

Riley raised her eyebrows. "Little? If she hasn't answered your calls in two days, I'd say it was more than little." Riley led them all into the kitchen and went about starting the kettle.

"How did you know it was two days?" Dane asked her, folding his arms over his chest. "He didn't say how long he'd been trying to get a hold of her, but you knew it was two days."

She opened her mouth then snapped it shut.

"Riley, I need to talk to her. Not just about us, but the case."

"Oh. The case." Riley raised her eyebrows.

"Not just for that reason. More because she ran out of my place the other day and hasn't answered me back. I've left messages, but she won't respond." He dragged his hand through his hair. "Yes, I am angry she's hiding from me, but more than that — I'm worried. There's a maniac out there and she's set on doing this herself. I can't let anything happen to her."

Riley sighed and rubbed her eyes. "And she gave me so much shit over running away from Dane. She's working the case." She pointed a finger at Dane. "She made me swear not to tell Tate if he showed up."

"Go on." Dane rolled his hand in the air. "What is she doing, that harebrained friend of yours."

"She went to the prison. To see the guy you arrested. His defense attorney is an old friend of ours from law-school, and she called her up asking a favor."

"We tried that, his attorney blocked us after he signed the confession."

"You, yes. Silvia understands Sydney's need to get this case right."

"Well, at least someone understands." Tate jammed his hand into his hair. "Because I sure as hell don't. She's obsessed with this case, with proving this guy didn't do it. I agree, he didn't, but she completely flew off the handle the other day because I took one step in the case without bringing her along. And when I ask her about why she's so incensed with it she changes the subject."

"She didn't tell you?" Dane looked at Riley then Tate. "She never mentioned her father?"

"Her father? No." They hadn't talked much about family at all really.

"She wouldn't," Riley said.

"What about her father?" Tate tried to keep his patience, but the longer this conversation took the more worried he became for Sydney.

"When she was in high school, her father was arrested for murder. It wasn't him, but he pleaded guilty to protect Sydney and her mother. The guy who was actually guilty had a shit ton of money and connections. Sydney's father had been at the same bar as the victim that night and when the cops started getting close to the real killer, he pinned it on Syd's dad. Then he went to visit her mom, and told her what would happen to her and Sydney if her husband didn't confess to the murder."

"None of the evidence, what little they had, pointed to Syd's dad, but the cops didn't want to work the case. Too easy to just grab him. And then when he gave his false confession, they just accepted it," Riley finished explaining.

Tate sighed and closed his eyes. "So now she makes sure only the guilty are actually prosecuted."

"Right. She won't go into defense work, because she won't defend the guilty, but she won't put an innocent person behind bars. Her father died in prison. He had a heart attack a month before his parole hearing."

"Oh fuck." Tate groaned. "She should have told me!"

"She should do a lot of things, but Sydney is stubborn and is positive she can take care of herself. If it needs doing, she'll take care of it. Why do you think she's off at the damn prison right now?" Dane asked.

"I'm going to take a layer off her ass when I get my hands on her."

"Didn't you break up with her?" Riley asked in her protective friend voice.

"What? No! Why the hell would I do that?"

"She said you did. She said you asked her how it could possibly work between you two."

Tate took another calming breath. Something he did a lot since meeting Sydney. "No. Well, yes but I didn't mean it that way. She... damn it. I'm going to go back over to her apartment and wait for her. If you hear from her, tell her I have important information about the case. Maybe then she'll answer my fucking call."

He didn't wait for a response; he just marched out of the apartment.

The woman thought he broke up with her? She'd lost what sense she possessed if she really believed he'd just let her go like that. One fight and it was over? No way.

But when he thought about what her father did, what she'd lost because of shitty police work, he understood so much more about her.

* * *

SYDNEY LEANED BACK on her couch, running her hand over her hair to smooth out the flyaways while sipping her second glass of moscato. The day had been long, but productive.

The police were tracking down the name Mr. Stanley had given them, Pickett. John had been right about one thing; the gym was the connection. But not between the girls and their killer. Pickett met Michael Stanley at the gym where they both worked out. They'd met for drinks a few times. After Pickett found out he had a small drug dealing business on the side, and his girlfriend was pregnant, he had what he needed. Someone to take the fall for him.

She had thought to call Tate herself, let him know what was going on, but she couldn't. She needed more time. So, like a coward, she'd called John.

Tate and she hadn't been together very long. His giving up on her, on them, really shouldn't hurt as much as it did. But even the wine wasn't dulling the pain in her chest when his name roamed into her mind. And it roamed, stampeded, jumped and pirouetted through every couple of minutes.

He'd left a few messages on her voice mail, but she'd ignored them. His text messages went unread. If it was something to do with the case, he'd call her office. Besides, with her out of his hair, he wouldn't have to worry about her getting involved.

Except the little voicemail icon on her phone kept glaring at her, and she ached to hear his voice again, to feel his arms wrapped around her. He was the first man to not shy away from her when she got an attitude. He hadn't walked away when her inner brat came out. Instead, he'd shown her how coming clean about what she wanted, being honest with herself, could open new doors for her. For them.

She threw back the last of the wine and went to the kitchen for a refill. She wondered what Tate thought about her solving the case. She had called John with the name Michael Stanley gave them. Scott Pickett, even his name made him sound like an ass. She avoided all questions about why she wasn't calling Tate and gave him the straight forward information, letting him know he'd have an arrest warrant ready to go by morning and to pick up the guy for questioning right away.

Her doorbell rang as she made her way back to her couch. Her forgiving, comforting couch. It would never dump her. It would always be reliable, sitting right in the middle of the living room waiting to lull her to sleep after she finished her bottle of wine.

The bell rang again. Her pizza. A few slices of sausage and mushroom along with another glass of wine, and she'd be ready to sink into her bed for a much-needed sleep. If she could get her mind to stop working.

"Coming!" She called, grabbing the cash for Tommy's tip from her purse on the armchair. She cursed when it fell over, spilling half the contents, but rushed to the door and flung it open. "Dominick?" She tucked the door as tight against her body as she could and looked down the hall. Empty. She should have checked the peep hole!

"Hey, Sydney. I, uh, actually I was hoping Tate would be here with you. Is he?" He stretched his neck to try and look over her head.

"No, he's not. Everything okay?" A knot formed in her stomach, and she held the door tighter, getting ready to slam it shut and bolt it.

His tie was half undone, his shirt wrinkled and his hair stood up in places like he'd been pulling at it.

"Yeah. Yeah." He nodded, rubbing his hands together. "I, uh, well I had this date tonight, and it went horrible. I was sort of hoping to talk to Tate. He's got a reputation at the club, you know, for being a bit of a lady's man, and I thought maybe I could pick his brain."

Lady's man? Tate? He played with plenty of subs before they started seeing each other but the description of him being a lady's man didn't fit what she knew of him.

"Well, he's not here. How did you get my address anyway?" she asked.

"Jaxson," he answered. "Do you mind if I come in? Maybe you can help me figure out what the hell went wrong tonight."

"Jaxson gave you my address?" The hairs on the back of her neck came to attention. She needed to get back inside, but she needed to keep him calm at the same time.

Dominick started fluttering his hands in his coat pockets. "Yeah. He said Tate could help me."

"You talked with Jaxson about talking to Tate, but got my

address?" She'd changed into her pajama pants when she got home. No pockets in pajama pants, and her cell was sitting on the coffee table. "Well, like I said. He's not here, so I have to—Dominick!" She tried to slam the door closed, but he lurched forward.

Something bit her in the neck, but she swung her arms out, knocking his hands away. Stumbling back into her apartment she tried to reach her phone, but her legs gave out from under her and she went down. Her head hit the laundry basket of freshly folded towels.

Ice cubes fell in the freezer. The TV clicked off. She tried to get up but her arms wouldn't work. She was too heavy. The room was foggy. When did all the fog roll in?

"Dominick," she said.

He laughed.

"Dominick, help."

He laughed louder. A hard kick to her ribs rolled her onto her back. "Help you? I am helping you."

"No." She blinked. Nothing was in focus.

Another sharp prick, to her arm this time. And the fog grew heavier until she couldn't see through it at all.

CHAPTER 16

"*What* the hell do you mean she called you?" Tate yelled into his cell phone as he slammed his car door. Getting to Sydney's apartment took twice as long thanks to a fucking accident clogging up the main road, and construction work blocked off the back roads he could have used.

"She called me. Said she got Michael to talk. We have an address for this Scott Pickett guy. You want to meet us over there? I'm heading there now with a few uniforms."

"Where is it?" He looked up at the building, the light in her living room burned bright. It wasn't even nine yet, she'd still be up working.

"111 Cranberry Street."

"That's way across town. I'll never get there in time. Just take him in, I'll meet you at the station in a few hours."

"Will do. Uh, I asked her why she didn't call you."

"Yeah? What did she say?" He could use the answer, too.

"She just said she couldn't." John rarely sounded sympathetic, especially when it came to a woman, but there it was.

"She could, she's just," he looked back up at the window, "she's just stubborn as a fucking mule. Call me when you get back to the station. I'm at her place now; once I talk with her, I'll head there."

"Got it."

The front door to the building was unlocked, again. He hated her building, the security sucked. If you could call the little panel with call buttons security. Not once had he needed to use it, the door was never locked and no one ever seemed concerned about it.

In the elevator, he thought about all the ways he could begin their discussion. The most common theme was to rip off her pants and bend her over his knee first thing. Maybe the arm of the couch, then he could use his belt with more accuracy.

An elderly woman stood in the hallway when he stepped off. He'd seen her before, one of Sydney's neighbors. She gave him a startled glance then looked down the hallway toward Sydney's apartment.

"Oh, I thought that was you earlier," she said.

"Me?" His stomach twisted.

"Well, I was wrong obviously. You are much larger, and your hair is darker."

"Larger than who?" His skin felt too tight for his body.

"The man carrying Sydney. Poor thing, she was so ill. He was taking her to the hospital."

"When was this?" He tried to soften his tone, but from the startled look she had, he had failed.

"Oh, half an hour I think. I was just going down to the laundry room."

He headed off down the hall at a sprint. Her door was closed, a pizza box sitting the floor in front of the closed door. The handle twisted freely and he pushed the door open. Pulling his gun from his holster, he looked around the living room. Nothing out of the ordinary, well except it was picked up. No dirty piles of clothes or excessive piles of mail on the tables. There was a basket of folded towels near the couch.

"Sydney!" he called running through the apartment, looking in the bathroom then her bedroom. Empty.

He ran back into the living room searching the room for a sign, a clue, something to tell him who the fuck had been there. The old woman had said he was a smaller build, lighter hair.

That could be fucking anyone in D.C.!

Nothing in the apartment was disturbed. Her cell phone sat on the coffee table, her purse half spilled on the arm chair in the corner as though she'd tossed it across the room. A full glass of that sickeningly sweet wine she loved sat on the coffee table, and the television was still on.

He dialed John, but it went to voice-mail. Frustrated he growled at the phone. *Think.* He needed to calm his mind for a minute and get back to the basics.

His phone rang and without looking at the screen he picked up the call.

"Sydney?"

"What? No, It's Wilkins. I have that name you wanted."

"Name?"

"Yeah, The Dom's real name. Or at least what he signed on his application. His real name is Scott Pickett."

"Fuck." Tate clenched his eyes closed. "Okay, thanks. Do you have a Sydney Richards listed as a member?"

"Uh, give me a sec." Keys tapped in the background before he came back to the phone. "No, but I do have her listed as a guest. A handful of times about a year ago."

"Was The Dom a member then?"

"No, his membership started six months ago. I told you, a newbie."

"Thanks." Tate hung up and dialed as fast as his fingers would fly across the touch screen.

"Hello." Jaxson picked up on the third ring.

"Jaxson! I need you to look up a member for me."

"Tate? What's going on? Hey, Emma, turn down the TV for a second." The background noise dropped off. "What's wrong?"

"I need you to look up a name. Is Scott Pickett a member?" Tate came right out and asked.

"Tate, I should probably—"

"I don't have time for any legal bullshit right now, Jaxson. She's gone. The fucker has her, I need you to look it up and see if he's a member and what his fucking tag name is."

"Okay, okay. Hold on."

More shuffling, but Tate could barely hear it over the thudding of his heart. He paced across the room.

"Sydney's missing?"

"She's gone. I think he took her, just please, get me the information." If anything happened to her, if she was badly hurt, or worse, he'd lose his mind. There would be no returning from that loss. He had to get to her.

"Pickett. Yes. He's a member. Shit. Wow. Uh, it's Dominick."

"What address does he have listed on his application?"

"111 Cranberry Street."

"I have that one already," Tate said.

"There's another one listed here. 125 R Street Northwest."

John was headed to the wrong place. "Thanks."

"You'll find her, Tate. She'll be okay." Jaxson sounded a hell of a lot more convinced than he felt at the moment.

"What would you do if someone took Emma from you?"

"I'd kill him with my bare hands."

"Exactly."

* * *

VOMIT. Sydney could smell it all around her. No matter which way she turned her head, there it was again. The second thing she noticed was the burning in her limbs. She tried to move, but nothing would do what she wanted.

Twisting, she realized her wrists were bound to her ankles behind her. The ropes bit into her flesh, which there was a lot of now that her clothes were missing, too. She wiggled more, the ropes moved, but didn't give enough for her to get her arms free.

Blinking, the room finally came into focus.

She wasn't just hogtied, she was tied to the ceiling as well. Laying belly down on a table, but trussed up like a neat package. Just like the two girls.

"Ah, she's finally awake!" That voice. That nasally, whiny little voice.

"D-Dominick." She coughed a few times, clearing her lungs. "What the fuck?"

"Oh, language!" A sharp slap hit her ass cheek. What the hell was he doing?

"Fuck you!" she yelled, her throat burning from the effort.

Another slap, this time to her back.

"You didn't think I was worth your time before, but I see I have your attention now."

"Attention? Is that what you wanted? Is that what you wanted with those girls?" She screamed, ignoring the biting pain in her throat.

He walked around her, coming to stand right in front of her. His eyes wild with anger, a raw fury she'd never seen before—an unbridled rage.

"Those little bitches thought they were too good for me. Too experienced to play with me. Thought they should just get their asses smacked and walk away, not giving me anything I wanted?" He slapped her across the face hard, her teeth snapping from the force. "Like you! Getting the spanking you asked for and all I wanted was a little pussy in return. But no, you hopped off that spanking bench, leaving me hard as fuck."

"Dominick, it had nothing to do with you. I don't fuck in the dungeon." Maybe playing into his ego would help, at least keep him engaged.

"Right. I saw you, not an hour later with that Neanderthals' fingers fucking you on the same damn bench I had you bent over. I got you wound up, and he gets the fucking homerun?"

His metaphors lacked as much skill as his dominance, but now was not the time to point that out.

"Just because he's got a little more experience. Well, we'll see how it goes this time!" His palm cracked against her cheek again.

She worked her jaw open and closed, working out the sting. When she righted herself, and could see him again, a knife appeared in her vision. A ragged edged hunting knife. She swallowed and watched it as he moved it from one hand to the other.

"I've been reading up on knife play." He talked as he walked around her, dragging the flat side of the blade along her skin. She held still. One jerk from her could mean a prick of the steel.

"Did you read up on spanking, too?" If her body could remain still, why couldn't her tongue?

"What, you didn't like my spanking?" His sarcasm made her believe he couldn't quite admit to himself how horrible he'd been that night. He seemed to see himself in a godlike fashion.

The knife appeared in her face again, the point of it pressing against her cheek.

"It, it was fine." She answered, keeping her eyes focused on the tip.

"That's what I thought."

"Do you understand the police know your real name? They are going to find you."

He laughed. "What they are going to find is an empty house. No furniture, no electricity. Nothing."

"They are going to find you," she said again. Tate would find him. He wouldn't give up until he did.

She wouldn't be in this mess if she'd just been less stubborn. If she'd taken his calls, texted him back. If she had called him instead of John to talk about Pickett, she wouldn't be trussed up on some table ready for carving.

"Oh, thinking your knight in shining armor is going to come save you?" He laughed again and an electric zap bit into her shoulder. He flicked the zapper in front of her face. "Do I start cutting, or should we have some fun first?" A zap to her bicep had her jumping but the ropes didn't give much.

"Your knight isn't coming." Zap. "He's never going to find you, either." Another jolt to her shoulder. He moved down the length of the table. "I've gotten a little smarter. Even if they do find you, they'll never figure out who you are." A jolt to the side of her stomach. She managed to keep her cries to herself.

She'd never get out of the situation if she lost her mind; she had to think straight. There had to be away out of his shitty bondage. She'd seen the pictures of the girls, he didn't know his knots well enough, but her arms and legs were still too heavy to move.

"Now now, no wiggling." A sharp prick to her shoulder, and a warm sensation ran down her arm. "There. It won't knock you out, unfortunately for you, but it will keep you from moving around so damn much."

Her head rolled to the side. She tried to lift it, to see what he came at her with, but nothing she did could get her body to listen to her. Everything was limp, and heavy, and hot. All her muscles just felt so damn hot.

Another jolt from the zapper to the side of her breast, and another to her stomach, her back, then her leg. He moved around her faster, poking her with the electric toy here and there. She wanted to scream, the little pin points of pain starting to increase with how long he held the device to her skin, how many times he struck the same place, but even her vocal cords abandoned her.

His laughter started to take over the room, and she wished for the fog again. She wanted the fog back.

"Oh, not such a smart ass now, are you?" He put his face up against hers. His breath reeked of garlic. Why had she ever thought him nice enough to play with? What the hell had she been thinking?

"Oh, she's still a smartass." Tate's voice rang through the room. She moved her eyes, searching for him, but nothing. Maybe she was completely delusional and hearing things.

Dominick scurried away from her, she could sense him close but not *as* close. She tried to talk, to call for Tate, but nothing worked yet.

"How'd you? What the fuck!"

Footsteps, several, and a fist hitting a jaw echoed in the room. A body crumpled to the floor and more growling and jumbled words were thrown around.

Nothing made sense. Tate was here? How could he be here? Had Dominick really left, or was he still here?

"Take this pathetic ass upstairs." Tate's voice again. The commanding, dominating voice she craved. Tears slipped from her eyes, then his hands were on her. Touching her head just before he came into view.

"Baby, I'm going to untie you now. Where do you hurt?"

She tried to talk, her lips moved, she could feel that, but nothing came out.

"What the fuck did he give you?" He disappeared, more shuffling. Drawers opened and slammed shut.

The ropes loosened and her arms and legs fell flat against the table.

"Can you move?"

She looked at him when he appeared again. She wanted to touch him, hold him, run into his arms, but she could only blink.

"I need a medic! Now!" He bellowed over his shoulder. "Now, Goddamn it!" He wiped the tear from her face. "It's going to be okay, we'll get you to the hospital, and you're going to be fine. Got me?" Smiling was too much for her, but she sighed. Tate was there and the killer was in cuffs. Finally, the fog came, blurring everything from her sight again.

CHAPTER 17

*T*he machines beeped too loudly. Tate leaned over them trying to find a volume control.

"What are you doing?" the night shift nurse demanded to know when she walked in the room. He straightened up and pointed to the beeping.

"It's too loud. It's going to wake her up. Make it softer."

"Make it softer?" She gave him an incredulous look, though she had done that so often when she talked with him over the past five hours he began to wonder if she just always looked that way.

"You're going to wake her up, and she needs sleep."

"With a bear like you for a husband, it's a wonder she ever fell asleep to begin with. You're making more ruckus than the machines. Now sit down." The little woman gave him a push to his chest and moved around the bed to finish what she came in for. She gave him another glare before clicking off the beeping machine and set about changing the IV bag.

"He's not my husband," a soft voice announced from the bed. Tate nearly knocked over the nurse to get to her side. She growled at him, a real growl, and shoved him out of her way, pointing to the other side of the bed.

"Well, if he's not now, he will be soon enough. This man has been hovering over you like the worst mother hen I've ever seen. And men only act that way when they can't think about life without their girl." The nurse felt Sydney's forehead. "Are you having any pain?"

"My head. It's achy, like cluttered."

"That's normal with all the drugs that were pumped into you. I'll call the doctor and let him know you're alert." She pointed a perfectly groomed finger at Tate. "You keep your voice down, and no smothering her, now. The doctor will be around in a bit to check her over."

Tate was about to respond to the cheeky nurse when Sydney giggled.

"You find her funny?" He tried to put a serious spin on his voice, but it was useless. She giggled again. "I think the drugs may have affected your brain too much."

"You found me." Her hand moved, covering his own.

"Damn right I did."

"I was scared, so scared."

His stomach clenched at the tenderness in her voice. "Me, too." He admitted, stroking her jaw. "When you weren't in your apartment..." His voice cracked, and he took a breath. "Fuck, Syd. I just about tore down all of D.C. to get to you."

"He was going to kill me."

"Never would have let that happen." The cold ran through his veins again. He would never forget the sight of her bound on that table, limp and drugged. If he could get his hands back on Dominick, he'd do more than just give him a few punches.

"I ignored you." A tear slid from one eye, and down her face. He caught it on his thumb when it reached her chin.

"Yeah, you did. But we can talk about all that later. Right now, you're going to do what the doctor says, you're going to get better, and you're going to come home with me."

"Home with you?"

"Yes, with me. My condo. Your building has shit for security, and besides, my place is cleaner." He squeezed her hand.

"You broke up with me." She sniffled.

"That only happened in your head. We had a fight, Sydney. Couples fight. Even couples like us."

She closed her eyes for a moment and when she opened them more unshed tears filled them. "I'm so sorry. About everything. Being obsessed about the case, not giving you a chance after I left your place, being so difficult about everything."

"Shh." He cradled her face in his hands and kissed the tip of her nose. "It's okay. All of it. Every bit of it is okay. And we'll talk about all of it, straighten it all out."

She licked her lips. "When you say straighten it all out?"

"I mean I'm going to lay into your ass like nothing you've ever had before." He said the words with a smile.

She laughed.

"I'm not kidding," he told her, but she laughed again.

"I know you're not. But I'm so sore, I can't imagine anything like that right now."

"Fine. I'll let you heal." He sighed dramatically and kissed her forehead. "But the moment you're all better, you can believe I'm putting a fire in your ass."

"Tate, you're going to smother her to death!" Riley's voice filled the room. "Sydney!" She ran around the bed, nudging him away. Apparently, every woman in the hospital thought they could just push him around.

"You're going to let her manhandle me like that?" he asked Dane when he stepped up to the bed. Riley was busy looking over Sydney, as though she had been handed a medical degree on the way up to the room.

"When it comes to Sydney, she's unreasonable. When it comes to each other, they both are." He looked past him at Sydney.

"Didn't I tell you *not* to go after him? Didn't I say it was a harebrained thing to do?" Riley released Sydney's face and plopped down on the bed.

"The mother hen is here. Tate can clock out," Sydney said, wincing and placing a hand on her head.

"What's the damage?" Dane asked.

Tate looked over at Sydney talking with Riley, a half smile on her lips and groggy looking eyes. She needed more sleep, a lot more sleep. And more fluids to flush out the crap Dominick had put in her system.

"Overall she's okay. Just need to flush out the drugs he gave her. Paralytics mostly."

"He's in custody?"

"Fuck, yes." Tate didn't get to have the honor of putting the cuffs on the bastard himself, but the few times his knuckles met his face was enough to console him over that fact.

"How the hell did you find her?"

Tate stepped further away from the bed. Sydney didn't need to hear everything; she needed rest.

"The address we had for him was a vacant home. The address he gave Black Light on his application was real. Can you believe the stupidity? Since Black Light does such a thorough check on backgrounds, he had to give both real addresses, or he wouldn't have gotten a membership."

"He probably figured you'd never figure out it was him and look at his records." Dane nodded.

"He was smart enough to have the decoy house," Tate pointed out. Sydney put on a brave front, smiling a little, but he could see the hurt there. Not just the physical pain, but the fear, the terror at what had almost happened to her.

"Thank God you got to her." Riley stepped to them.

Tate looked back at the bed, Sydney had fallen back asleep.

"She needs sleep," he said and headed back to her. "Why don't you two head home. She'll call you in the morning."

"No way. I'm staying." Riley started to take off her jacket, but Dane grabbed it and draped it back over her shoulders.

"We'll just be in the way, here, Riley. She's okay. He'll call us in the morning, and we'll come back. Right now, let's just get home."

"I'll be quiet. I'll sleep on the little couch right there. Why are you shaking your head?"

"Sometimes I really need to draw it out for you, don't I?" He grabbed her elbow. "We'll see you in the morning," he said to Tate as he led Riley out of the room.

The little couch was accounted for, and the recliner. He wasn't leaving the room until Sydney went with him. And not even Nurse Ratched would be able to get him to move before then.

He had his girl back. No fucking way he was going to even blink until she was at his condo where he could keep his eyes on her.

CHAPTER 18

"I'm not sure this is really necessary." Sydney walked over to the St. Andrew's cross where Tate had a table laid out with several implements. "I'm feeling much better, less stressed now that the trial is over."

Tate stopped digging through his duffel bag to shoot her a quick look expressing perfectly what he thought of her statement. Total bullshit.

"Fine." She shrugged and stripped out of her dress. Summer had finally arrived and was in full swing. The heat from the sun kept her in her favorite cotton dresses. Turned out Tate loved them as well, quickly dictating she was to fill her wardrobe with them immediately.

"Are you going to play like you aren't looking forward to this? Or are you going to admit that you are?" He stilled, his hands still buried in his bag.

She knew what he wanted. The same thing he always wanted. The full truth, nothing but, so help her ass. "Of course, I'm looking forward to this." She rolled her eyes and walked up to the table, picking up his favorite flogger and running her fingers through the leather falls. "Other than that little punishment I got once the doctor gave me the all clear, you've been treating me like some glass ornament."

"Little punishment?" He cocked a brow. Okay, it had been the worst to date, but since then, he'd barely given her a hard lash of any belt or flogger.

"It wasn't little. I know that." She lowered her chin when she made her confession. "I nearly cost us everything."

He turned from the bag and pulled her in his arms. "No more talk like that, Syd. It's over, and we are back on the right track, right?"

"Yes, sir." She sighed and leaned into his chest. The warmth of his body and the softness of his shirt soothed her. As frustrated as she'd been with his easy treatment of her, knowing he was going to have her strung up on the cross for an evening of whatever he had planned still made her nervous.

"You're shaking."

"I'm just cold." She pulled out of his arms and showed him the little bumps running over her skin. "They have the AC cranked up, and I'm naked—in case you haven't noticed." She put a hand on her hip.

He laughed. "Oh, I fucking noticed. Now get your little ass over on the cross, I found my cuffs."

She stepped up onto the circular, wood platform and stood beneath the lighting. The wait was short. He joined her quickly and started to wrap the black leather cuffs around each wrist and ankle. One more trip to his bag and he had a few short chains. She wasn't exactly tall enough to reach the rings on the top of the cross, so he hooked the chains to her wrist and then the top rungs. By the time he was finished, her legs were spread wide, her arms were overhead, and her ass was perfectly on display.

"Your hair is too long, I think it's time for a cut."

"It's not too long. Let me down and I'll put it up in a bun."

He laughed. "And lose my leash? Hell no." He wrapped the thick locks around his fist and pulled her head back until her neck was completely exposed. Leaning down, he kissed her mouth, then her chin, and moved further down until he was sucking on her neck, biting and then licking. When he released her, her mind spun and the butterflies fluttering around her stomach eased into a harmonious dance.

"Now, I won't gag you, but if you start getting mouthy you know I will." His breath was hot against her ear. Her hair was pulled back again.

"Are you braiding my hair?" She asked the question without trying to look.

"I am capable of such a feat, yes." He tied off the bottom and threw the long braid over her shoulder, keeping the entire back side of her body exposed. "Now, keep your mouth shut." He kissed her neck again, then bit her shoulder. She sank into the sensation of his teeth on her bare skin, sighing with the heightened sensation.

"Yes, sir," she whispered when he released her. The chill of the room washed across her back, but soon was replaced with his finger stalking down her back. First the pads of his fingertips, then the sharp tips of his nails as he dragged them from her shoulder to her ass, then up from her ass to her shoulders.

"You like that?" he asked, grabbing her ass in two hard grips.

"Yes, sir."

"You love it?"

"Fuck, yes." She nodded.

He chuckled. "Of course you do, my little pain slut."

Six months ago, she would have railed against him using such a term. But six months ago, she hadn't had him at the helm. He hadn't been the one holding the flogger or the dragon tail, giving her every bite, every burn the implement could offer.

"We haven't used the leather flogger in a while, but first I think five with the wooden paddle."

"What?" She pulled against the cuffs "Why?" Wood was kept solely for punishment.

"Because it's what I want," he said simply, as he returned to the platform with the small hairbrush-shaped paddle in hand.

"I hate wood," she pouted.

"Too bad, I think." He slid his arm between her body and the cross, holding her around her hips. "Push this delicious ass out for me. I want a good target."

She wanted to huff. It wasn't fair, but she did as she was told because after the wood came the flogger, and then came heaven.

He made no ceremony of it either, five hard strokes to each cheek in rapid succession. Her brain screamed from the sudden current of electricity, and she hopped from one foot to the other. "You said five! That was ten!"

The paddle rubbed across her ass "You have two cheeks, Sydney. Five on each cheek. Now you'll get two more because you got all mouthy. Don't forget, I have the ball gag with me. I know how much you love to stand in the corner and have your drool cover your tits."

She hated that. Not in the it-was-hot sort of way, but in the hell-no-she-wasn't-doing-that sort of way. She clamped her mouth shut and took the next four strokes better. Biting her lip to keep from snarling at him.

"Now, we can get to the flogger." He kissed her shoulder. "You did good, babe." He used the paddle to tap her ass.

When he returned, she rested her head on the beam of the cross, waiting for him to begin with the light little flickers over her ass and back. Instead, two fingers thrust up into her and she cried out from the sudden fullness.

"Fuck you're wet. Did you fuck yourself earlier like I told you to?"

He'd taken to making her come before they went out to play.

"Yes, sir." She had, just like he told her to, with his vibrator, on his bed, fully dressed from the top up.

"Good girl. Did you come?"

"No, sir," Getting to the edge of heaven and pulling back was a cruel task to make her perform, but she had to admit it did make the spankings more enjoyable when he finally got around to playing with her

His fingers were gone, but too soon the pleasant sensation was replaced by the bite of the falls crossing her shoulder blades. She hadn't been ready, but the second swing she stood firm.

He kept a steady rhythm, keeping to her back and her ass. Soon he ramped up his swings harder and harder until she grunted with each stroke. The tips of the falls bit into her, contrasting the thump of the leather with the bite of the ends. He became unpredictable. Thuddy, heavy, soft, sharp—every sensation started to blend into the other.

Nothing existed outside of their little platform. The giggles and screams of the other subs having their asses beat or fucked, melted away. The club wasn't surrounding them. Nothing was. It was just them.

"Goddamn, I've missed that." His chin rested on her shoulder. She nodded, unable to use her mouth for much at the moment. "Color?" He dug his nails into her ass again.

"Yellow," she whispered. She could go longer, but he wouldn't. Once she hit yellow, or he thought she should be at yellow, he backed off. Never giving her too much, but always giving just enough.

"Such a good girl." He pressed against her ass, his erection grinding against the hot soreness of her flesh.

"Fuck me, Tate. Please fuck me!" She looked over her shoulder.

"The privates are all being used."

"Here. Fuck me right here."

He stood seemingly stunned for a moment then asked, "Are you sure?"

"Yes!" she nearly screamed.

He laughed and walked way. When he returned, his pants were gone and he was rolling a condom over his long, thick shaft. She nearly wept for joy at seeing his cock pointed at her.

"Sometimes I wonder who you think is in charge around here." He grabbed her ass and thrust up into her pussy with one feverish stroke.

She yelped, but arched her back to give him more of her ass. He gripped her waist and thrust into her. '

"You! You're in charge," she said.

"Really? So, if I say you can't come?"

His voice already ragged, his breathing already hard, he was as close as she was.

"I won't come then." She wouldn't. She'd hate it, but she'd follow his order.

"Fuck."

His cock thrust harder, farther into her body as she began to meet him thrust for thrust.

"I have to. Can I? Now, I have to now!" She yelled filling the dungeon with her passionate sounds, unaware of anyone around them.

"Yes, come now. Oh fuck!"

And together they cried out as their orgasms ripped through them.

When he pulled out, she went limp against the cross, resting her head on the beam and pressing her weight into the fixture. He kissed her head and told her to relax while he cleaned them up.

After taking her down from the cross, he wrapped her in a blanket and brought her to a couch nearby. "Stay right here." His order came with a soft kiss to her forehead. Her ass hurt, her back hurt, but watching him jog back over to their station and gather up their toys, her heart felt full.

After he wiped down he cross, and zipped up his bag he jogged back over to her. "Here." He handed her a bottle of water and sat next to her on the couch, pulling her into his lap.

She held onto the bottle of water, deliberating.

After several silent moments stretched past, she looked at him.

His brow creased when she remained silent, but she soothed it away with a brush of her fingertips across his jaw.

"I love you," she said with a nod.

His lips tugged a little at the edges, then broke into a full grin.

"I already knew that." He kissed her, a quick peck. "Just took you a little while to know it, too."

"You love me, too," she announced and snuggled back into his chest.

His chest vibrated when he chuckled and his arms went tighter around her. "I already knew that, too."

"You never said it." She yawned.

"Not with words, no. But I'll say it now, and every day. I love you."

She sighed. "See, I told you."

"Brat." He pinched her ass.

Sometimes she would be, and he'd let her play for a minute. But she didn't need to act out to get what she wanted. Tate would always know, would always fulfill her every fantasy and desire. Because that's what you do when you're in love. You lean on each other. You fill each other's day with joy. No games needed.

Besides. She'd already won.

She had Tate.

And Tate had her.

THE END

ABOUT THE AUTHOR

Measha Stone is an international bestselling author of erotic romance. She's had #1 top-selling books in BDSM, and suspense. She lives in the western suburbs of Chicago with her husband and children, who are just as creative and crazy as her. Her vanilla writing has been published in numerous literary magazines, but she's found her passion in erotic romance.

Contact Measha
https://www.meashawrites.com/blog

ALSO BY MEASHA STONE

Windy City Series

Hidden Heart

Secured Heart

Indebted Heart

Liberated Heart

Protecting His Pet

Black Light: Valentine Roulette

BLACK COLLAR PRESS

Did you enjoy your visit to Black Light? Have you read the other books in the series?

Infamous Love, A Black Light Prequel by Livia Grant
Black Light: Rocked by Livia Grant
Black Light: Exposed by Jennifer Bene
Black Light: Valentine Roulette by Various Authors
Black Light: Suspended by Maggie Ryan
Black Light: Cuffed by Measha Stone
Coming Soon: Black Light: Rescued by Livia Grant

Black Collar Press is a small publishing house started by authors Livia Grant and Jennifer Bene in late 2016. The purpose was simple - to create a place where the erotic, kinky, and exciting worlds they love to explore could thrive and be joined by other like-minded authors.

If this is something that interests you, please go to the Black Collar Press website and read through the FAQs. If your questions are not answered there, please contact us directly at: blackcollarpress@gmail.com.

WHERE TO FIND BLACK COLLAR PRESS:

- Website: http://www.blackcollarpress.com/
- Facebook: https://www.facebook.com/blackcollarpress/
- Twitter: https://twitter.com/BlackCollarPres

LET US KNOW WHAT YOU THINK

The art of writing can be a lonely activity at times. Authors sit alone, pouring their hearts into their stories, hoping readers will connect with their words and fall in love with their characters. It's easy to get discouraged at times.

And that's where you come in.

We'd sure appreciate it if you'd take a few minutes to leave a review to let us know what you thought of the story you just finished.

Thanks and happy reading!

Jennifer, Livia & Measha

Made in the USA
Columbia, SC
02 March 2020